Defending Her Honor

Copyright

Opening Quote

Whiskey glass on the mattress. I ain't slept since you left. You ain't coming back again. I still see them Goodyears spinning. Little gravel, dust slinging. Tail lights beaming on a self-centered prick with a problem who's dealing with the cost of... Living my life going through hell 'cause the bourbon ain't working. You probably would've never loved me if you could see all the bridges I'm burning. Tears in your eyes. You saw the truth from the lies. No saving you from what became to be the villain in me.

Villain In Me by Ryan Jesse

Chapter One

❦ Dylan ❦

I'm already in love with Chicago. Kingston University is my favorite place in the city, but I love the entire ambiance that is Chicago. I just arrived here a couple of days ago, but I've already decided it's home. It's where I'm meant to be. It helps that two of my best friends in the world are here. I hate that I had to leave my cousins behind in Brystone Springs, Texas, but I can still see them and talk to them whenever I want to. Chicago is what I've always dreamed of.

Not that it was the goal my parents had for me. They both told me I'd be going to the University of Texas. That was their plan for me. Whenever I brought up Chicago and all of the benefits of Kingston University, I was immediately shot down. It didn't seem to matter that Kingston University is in the top ten colleges in the nation and ranks in the top twenty around the entire world. They had their plan, and that was final.

I applied anyway because that's what my cousins pushed me to do. They said I'm becoming an adult. I can do what I want, and if my dad cuts me off, we'd figure it out together. I trusted them then just like I do now. Fortunately, my dad seems to be really on board with this. My mother, not so much.

I look at my clock when I finish getting ready. I'm really excited. Today is the day I get assigned my dorm room, and I might even get a special exception to move in early. If I don't, then Xavier, my oldest cousin, said he'd make sure I'm taken care of and put up somewhere for a couple of months. I've never been on my own, but this is the most exciting thing I've ever done, including winning the National Cheerleading Competition three times in a row for Brystone Springs High School.

I'm really excited to continue cheerleading for Kingston University. They're highly competitive and have a nationally recognized and ranked college football team. I have to go to tryouts, but I'm confident I can get on the team. It's another thing I'm super excited to talk about with the administration today.

I pick up my phone with a giant smile when it notifies me that my Lyft is outside the hotel I'm staying in. I hurry to the elevator after messaging him and saying I'm on my way down. A short ride later, I walk briskly to the exit of the hotel.

"I don't fucking care, ma'am. She's my responsibility. What room?"

I glance at the front desk and see a man standing there with his back to me. He's wearing biker cuts, and I'm pretty sure I recognize them. I remember my cousin, Drake, was talking about the Ruthless Warriors. The patches on his cuts have a patch that says Ruthless Warriors, so I hurry to leave. I don't know much about them, but I remember Drake's boyfriend saying they were bad news.

The hotel receptionist glances at me, and the man turns quickly. I put my head down just as fast and hurry outside to the Lyft waiting for me. I get in the back and lock the door swiftly. The driver seems like a nice younger man who is probably just doing this on the side.

"There's a riot happening just a few blocks away, so we'll have to change your route to get to the university."

"Oh, that's okay. I appreciate that." I glance nervously at the hotel door when it opens. The man looks around until his dangerous, nearly black eyes land on me just as the driver pulls away from the curb and takes off.

Wide-eyed, I look behind us and watch in both shock and horror as the man, with someone else standing at his side, runs into the street like he's chasing us. It looks like he thinks better of it, though. He turns and runs the opposite direction, but it doesn't ease me at all. My heart is racing.

What the hell is happening? What does this person want with me? Is he chasing me?

I take my phone out and call Xavier, the only person I can think of right now. When he doesn't answer, I try again, and then a third time.

"My name is Landon, by the way. I know it says that in your app, but I like to make it formal," the driver, Landon, says to me.

"Nice to meet you, Landon. I'm Dylan." I take a deep breath and glance behind us as Landon turns and drives past an incredible amount of emergency vehicles and blacked out SUVs. I'm sure this is where the riot is happening, but my mind isn't on that. It's on how slowly he's going. I don't see anything, but I feel like I'm being chased.

"You're welcome to a water or energy bar if you like. There's a few in the seat back in front of you."

"I appreciate that. Thank you." I try calling Xavier again as I watch behind us. My eyes widen, and I slink down in my seat when I see a car coming towards us. It wouldn't bother me, except I can clearly see the driver is the man from the hotel. "Oh my God," I murmur.

"Hey, you okay? Don't worry about the riot. We'll get through it. No problem."

"It's not that, Landon. I, uh… I think we're being followed. And… I don't know who it is, but I saw them at the hotel when I was leaving. They ran out as you were pulling out."

I watch his eyes darken as he glances in his rearview mirror. Protective instincts seemingly drop over his entire physique. "Okay. We don't panic until we know for sure. If he tries something, I'll drive towards a district station. Hopefully, not all the cops are at the riot."

I blink as the word 'riot' finally sinks in. "Oh my God," I mumble again. "How are you so calm? What is this riot?" I call Xavier a fifth time.

"Last week, some cop shot an unarmed man. He was Black, so there's a lot of speculation behind why it happened. A lot are calling it racially motivated, and it seems that way. There was a video released that showed the whole thing. The man didn't resist at all. He got shot execution style. The department has been very quiet about it. Some news station reported the cop's name, even though the department hadn't made any kind of a statement regarding who it was. They only said they were investigating it. I guess after he was identified, people got pissed and called for action. Somehow, it was assumed he was on administrative leave, but he wasn't. It's a pretty big mess. I think a lot of people are making things up." He speeds up when he hits the Freeway. "I guess I'm so calm about it because I'm sure the truth will come out in the end. There's too many unanswered questions for all this."

I look behind us again. "He's getting closer."

"We stay calm," he says to me.

I shakily call Colton, Xavier's husband. "Please, please pick up," I whisper.

"Hey, gorgeous. How's Chicago?"

"Where's X?"

"Shower. What's up? You sound shaky."

I take a deep breath. "I am. I'm in a Lyft right now on my way to campus to get into my dorm room. There's a riot in Chicago. Something about a cop allegedly killing an unarmed guy. Oh, and did I mention I'm being chased by someone? I don't know who, but I swear the cuts were Ruthless Warriors."

"Jesus Christ. Did you say riot? And chased?"

"What?" I hear Xavier say.

"Hang on. I'll put you on speaker." There's some shuffling. I'm terrified to poke my head up anymore. "Okay, now say that again. Xavier is here, too."

"There's a riot going on in the city. My Lyft driver is taking me to campus, and we're past the riot. It's slightly scary knowing there's a riot happening only blocks away from where I'm staying. It's over a cop allegedly shooting someone who was unarmed, but that's not the scariest thing. When I was coming down from my room, I heard some commotion by the desk. Someone asking where 'she' was or something. That she was his responsibility. I know hotels can't give information like that without the person being on the reservation or something. I didn't pay too much attention until I noticed the cuts. They were Ruthless Warriors, Colt."

"Fuck," Xavier says.

"I didn't know who they were there for, but the receptionist glanced so very briefly at me. She looked terrified, and that second was all it took for the man to look at me, too. I hurried out and got in the car. I locked the door. The driver took off very quickly. The man came out with another guy just as my driver was taking off. They ran a little into the street before running back towards the sidewalk. When we got to where the riot is, I saw we were being followed by the same men in a car."

"A car? What kind of car? Can you see the plate?"

"No. To all of that. The car is black. Looks a little bit like the car from *Supernatural*, but I really don't know, and I'm too afraid to look. I don't want them to ram us."

"They're coming up on the side of us," Landon interrupts.

"Get on the floor, Dylan. Face down," Xavier says to me.

I don't hesitate. I drop to the floor behind the driver's side seat and make myself as small as possible. "What do I do? The police have to be busy with this riot."

"Tell your driver to keep driving towards the University. Campus police will be there. Tell him to drive to them," Colton says.

"Colt said go to the campus police, Landon. He's a detective in Brystone Springs, Texas."

"You got it. Campus police are in the Administration building. At least they were. I graduated last year, and they were doing some remodeling. I don't know if they moved."

"Okay," I say.

"He's going back behind us. Still following."

Colton sighs at Landon's words. "Fuck."

"I'm calling Josh," Xavier says.

"Almost to campus." Landon turns off at an exit.

"Please just get me as close as you can," I tell him.

"X is on the phone with Josh, sweetheart. Just hang in there, okay? Get to the campus police. Stay there until he gets there."

"Get on the passenger side. I'm going to pull up in a circular driveway. It's closer to pull behind the cars then next to the two who are double parked. You won't be able to get out anyway. It's too narrow. I'm going to have to go up on the side to get out."

"Okay." I maneuver my way to the other side and sit back up on the seat, keeping my head low.

"Run as soon as he stops, Dylan," Colton commands.

"We're here," I say, feeling him slow down and turn but not seeing much since I'm still ducked down. "He said to run as soon as you stop."

"Okay. Campus police's office was right off to the right after you go in. Administration office is straight ahead," Landon says just as he stops.

"Thank you. Thank you so much." Tears start to sting my eyes as I leap out of the car and run.

There's no way to get by his car and the bushes that border the sidewalk, so I run right through them. The sticks and thorns scratch me, but I keep moving. The second I'm through, I hit a hole and fall. I can feel something in my ankle stretching unnaturally. A scream escapes me, but I refuse to give up. I grip my phone in my hand, though I'm sure it's broken.

"Go! Get her!" someone barks from behind me.

"No! No!" I screech when I feel hands on my arms pulling me up.

"It's me! Run!"

I look up and see Landon. He pulls me with him. My ankle burns, but I won't give up. I can't. "Ow!" I scream when my ankle gives out near the door.

Landon's arm is around my waist, and he's suddenly pushing me through the door. With renewed strength, I fight through the pain and sprint as fast as I can into the building.

"Shit!" Landon yells in frustration. The lobby is covered in plastic. Where he said the campus security would be is blocked off. He propels me to the Administration office.

I glance behind me as I enter and don't feel him near me anymore. My eyes widen when I see both men hauling him away from me.

He's fighting them. "Go!"

"Oh my God," I whisper. I disappear into the office, following his orders as I choke down a sob.

There are a lot of people in here. No one pays any attention to me or the commotion going on outside. I know I won't be getting any help for a while, and I don't want to cause a panic. It will do nothing but create more victims. Instead, I try closed office doors. They're all locked except one near the end of the row. I slip into it, thankful it's dark. I quickly lock the door.

"Colt," I whisper. I hurry to hide under the desk. My phone's screen is shattered, just as I thought it would be. I'm sure it happened during the fall, but all I can do is hope he can still hear me.

"I'm here! What the fuck is happening?"

"I'm in the admin building." The tears finally break free. "They got Landon!" I scream, still whispering.

"Fuck. Fuck, tell me you got Josh, X," Colton says.

"He's on the way. Keep hidden, Dylan. Where are you?" Xavier asks me, worry in his voice.

"I'm in an office in the Admin building. It's under construction. No campus police here."

"Where's RW?"

"They were dragging Landon somewhere. Xavier, I think they're going to kill him!" I choke on a sob and put my hand over my mouth to stay as quiet as possible.

"Fuck," Colton whispers. "Okay. Josh is on the way. Stay quiet. Stay hidden. Stay on the line with us."

"Yes, sir," I whisper. I clutch my phone to my chest wide eyed when I hear the door handle moving. "Someone's trying to get in!" I hiss into my phone as I close my eyes. I hold my breath and stay as still as possible until it stops.

"Ssh… Don't talk." Colton's voice is muffled since the phone is against my chest again, but I can make out what he says. I nod, even though he can't see me, and stay just like that until I hear someone talking on the phone again.

"Dylan? Still there?" Xavier asks.

"Mmhmm," I barely hum.

"He's there. Josh is there."

My eyes snap open. "Where?"

"In the admin office. He said there's someone standing outside a door not wearing cuts. He's wearing a blue shirt and Khaki shorts. Tan."

"Oh my God. Landon?"

"Josh isn't approaching because he doesn't know where you are and doesn't want to cause alarm. He already has enough attention on him. Is that what Landon was wearing?"

"Yeah, but I watched him being dragged away."

"Josh is there, Dylan. Trust him. Is there a window? Can you see out of it?"

I take a breath and quietly crawl out from under the desk. I can hear my heart in my ears. "There's no window," I whisper.

"He's out there," Colton says. "Can you see through the keyhole? Even if you can't, open the door. Josh is there. He'll protect you."

I hurry to the door, remaining as silent as possible. I do my best to see through the keyhole, and what I see makes my heart skip several beats. "It's him," I say tearfully as I unlock the door. I quickly stand and fling open the door. "I thought you were dead," I whisper to Landon.

"No, I got away after punching them both almost out cold and got in here, but these guys out here are looking at me. Go back in the office. I know who one of them is, but I don't know why he's here. I'll ask the desk to call the campus police."

"It's okay. They're here to help." I watch as Josh motions me to him. Landon follows. As soon as I reach Josh, I hug him. "I'm so glad you're here."

"We didn't find him," Josh says, hugging me back. "No one out there with your car description. Who is this?"

"They had to have left. They followed us the whole way here." I turn to Landon. "This is Landon. He was the Lyft driver."

"Nice driving," Josh says. "I hate to be a dick, but there's no way you can just go back to life until this is over."

Landon glances at me. "What the hell did I just get into?" He looks up at Josh. "You're Josh Lucinio. Mafia boss. Who were those guys?"

"Ruthless Warriors. We don't know why they're after her, though." Josh looks around at the nearly silent room before glancing at Gavin. "We should get out of here."

"Yeah, couldn't agree more." He shoots a glare at everyone and shoves the door open.

"I don't think they're gone," Josh says. "I think they're watching."

"Obviously, she needs to be protected at all costs," Landon says, following us.

"Uh, yeah. Exactly." Josh glances back at him. "Goes for you, too. You just made yourself a target, kid."

Landon shrugs. "Don't care about me. It's her that matters. We need to get her out of here. I'll worry about myself."

Josh eyes him for a few moments before nodding and looking down at me. "Out the door, and straight to the SUV ahead of us. No driver. It'll be me and Gavin. Understand?"

I nod as Gavin moves to my side. "I can't go back to my hotel."

"You're not going to," Gavin says. "We'll have a couple of guards get your stuff, but you're not going back."

"Why is this happening to me?"

"I don't know, Dylan," Josh says. "We'll figure it out once you're safe. Let's move."

I feel a hand on my back as we start running to the vehicle. Once I'm shut safely inside, Gavin gets in the passenger's seat. I put my phone back up to my ear. "They have me."

"Good. Call us later," Xavier says.

"I will."

Josh pauses at my door as I hang up. "Want a job? It pays better than Lyft. I pay your insurance, train you, and give you shelter and food."

"Work for the mafia?"

Josh chuckles. "Think about it. Get in the SUV behind us. You'll be going to our compound until we figure out what the fuck to do. I'll house you with the guards."

"I don't need to think about it, sir. I got kicked out of my apartment because I can't pay rent. I haven't been able to find a job in my field. I'm living in my car."

"What's your field?"

"Tech."

"I can always use tech people. Get in."

"Yes, sir." Landon hurries to the other SUV as Josh runs to the driver's seat of the one I'm in.

"First thing, we're going to get your stuff and get you checked out of your room," Josh says as he pulls out.

"Are you giving him a job?" I ask.

"If he wants it. Gav, get her ankle dealt with. She was barely able to make it out of there without me taking most of her weight. It looks pretty swollen."

I look down at it. "I forgot about it," I almost whisper.

Gavin leans forwards and pulls up a black bag. "Put your foot on the center console."

I do as I'm told and close my eyes, suddenly more than a little exhausted. I'm not even sure what happened or how. It all feels like a dream.

No. Not a dream.

A living, breathing nightmare.

Chapter Two

🍎 Cole 🍎

"How do you expect me to trust you after all of this stuff?" Carmella, my girlfriend of over a year asks.

I lean against the doorframe of my front door with my arms folded over my chest. "How about just trusting I'd never do anything so fucking heinous as kill another man in cold blood? Or has our entire relationship been based on sex and some kind of fantasy instead of love and commitment? Honesty. Trust. You know. Normal for relationships stuff."

Carmella looks down at the box of her stuff in her hand and shakes her head. "It's not that easy, Cole. You're all over the news. 'Cole Westwood, Sergeant with Chicago PD, suspended amid investigation'. And that's just the tame ones." She looks up at me, teary. "Do you understand what this can do to me and my reputation?"

I glare down at her. "Yeah. Sure I can see that. Obviously, that's more important than me or us. Which is why you have that box in your hand." I nod to it.

"Maybe when this blows over -"

"No. Nope. You made the choice."

"But -"

"No, Carmella. You've made your decision. If you really wanted anything between us to work out, we wouldn't be here right now."

She sighs and looks up at me one more time. "I'm not going to come back, then. It's really over this time."

"Okay." It's been over for a long time. I just never let myself admit it because the sex was so good. It's gonna be hard giving that up.

"You're such an asshole. I just think maybe time -"

"You've chosen to walk away when it gets hard. Instead of believing in me, the man you've been with for over a year, you're watching the news and thinking completely of yourself and how this will make you look."

"Cole, I could lose my job!" she yells, though quietly. She's always been all about appearances. She'll scream at me behind the walls of my house, but if anyone else has even a small chance of seeing her carefully manufactured persona crack, she crumbles.

I laugh. "Right. News reporter. Can't have your image tarnished with the likes of a bad cop."

"Cole, it's not just a bad cop. You're being charged with murder!" She looks around to make sure no one is looking out their windows or walking around or anything.

"One more thing being reported that isn't true, Carmella. Something you could set straight. I'm not being charged with anything." At least not yet. Who the fuck knows how long that will last.

She shakes her head. "Whatever. So, now all I'm good for is getting the media on your side."

I shrug indifferently. "I never said that. Couldn't hurt, though."

"Fuck, I can't believe how stupidly arrogant you are. I'm not coming back this time. I'm not. Once I leave, we're done."

I shrug again, just as indifferently. "Okay."

"Oh my God! Can you honestly just show some kind of emotion?"

"What the hell do you want me to say, Carmella? You're the one leaving. Not me."

"You could show you care a little about the breakup! Can't you at least try to be slightly upset and regretful?"

That gets a laugh out of me. "You want me to be upset with you for breaking up with me? Regretful that I fucked up somewhere, though I

15

don't know where, nor do I even give a shit? You're the one who wants to leave. So? Leave."

"God, you're so fucking stubborn and uncaring."

Another shrug. "Okay."

"Ugh!" She spins on her red high-heels and storms to her tiny as fuck car. A small, green, Cooper S two-door. I can't even get into the fucking thing.

I watch her small frame open the back hatch of the car. She's dressed in a short black skirt with nylons and a white blouse. Her blonde hair is done in a perfect updo, and her makeup is thick. I don't need to even ask to know she's going to work. If she weren't, she'd be wearing just as much makeup with some kind of ratty sweatpants. She rarely likes to get dressed up for me, and I don't ask for much. Put a pair of jeans or shorts on once in a while. Fuck.

She puts her box in the back of her car and closes the hatch. Her perky ass moves in tandem with the rest of her. It's her second best feature. The first is her mouth when it's around my cock. Better than her talking because her whiny voice is her worst feature.

She turns and looks at me, her green eyes welling with tears that have absolutely no effect on me. "I really hope you're cleared."

"Okay." One more shrug of indifference. She shakes her head and hurries to get inside her car. She meets my eyes in the rearview mirror as she turns it on and speeds away, nearly hitting an SUV when it turns into my driveway.

I don't move a single inch. My stance remains the same. I see Josh is driving, and Gavin is in the passenger seat. That's unusual in and of itself, but the past thirty-one hours have been fucked up anyway. Being arrested for the murder of an unarmed man is bad enough. Throw in that he was Black, and everyone lost their minds. A riot started. Two, actually. One was at the Headquarters building downtown where I was being detained. The other was here.

On *my fucking* home turf.

All because some video came out showing some guy in a uniform pulling a vehicle over, pulling him out shortly after, then shooting him. It was absolutely not justified. No one I've talked to in my department could see who it was. No one believes what they saw happen. Everyone thinks it's CGI or some shit. Our tech department was looking at it and trying to figure it all out.

That was the last thing anyone heard about it until I got pulled over by my own department and removed from my vehicle at gunpoint on an arrest warrant we found out very quickly was completely faked. It was issued by a deputy who doesn't exist and signed by a judge who's dead. The DA doesn't want to press charges. We kept everything quiet, so when the riot happened, we all knew someone leaked something to the press.

The questions now are who and why.

Josh steps out of the driver side as I watch. He looks pissed. Gavin doesn't look any happier, but he schools his anger as he opens the back door of the SUV. He helps a girl who can't be more than sixteen out of it. She looks like she's had a rough night. Her hair is a mess, and she has some kind of a brace on her foot. She's pretty scratched up. Almost like she went rolling down a hill of sticks and hit every single one of them on the way.

It's when I see duffel bags being pulled out behind her that my hackles are instantaneously raised. "No," I growl. "Whatever the fuck this is, no."

Josh glares as Gavin grabs the duffel bags. He puts an arm around the girl, his eyes darkening even more. "Yes."

I return the glare just as viciously, still not budging. "No."

"You don't have a fucking choice, Westwood," Josh growls. The mafia boss inside him is definitely coming out to play, but I've known him too fucking long to be intimidated.

"I just had the worst fucking day of my life, Lucinio. And that's including the day I got to Jessa in the hospital." I know as soon as the words are out of my mouth that I went way too far.

Before I can stop him, his hands are gripping my shirt, and I'm being slammed against my door. "I don't fucking care how much of a prick you want to be right now, and I understand the past thirty hours have been intense. Talk like that to me again, and I'll kick your ass. Blood, friend, family, or not."

"I'm sorry," I instantly apologize with both hands up in surrender. "I'm tired. Pissed. I shouldn't have said that. I'm sorry, Josh. Really. It was out of line."

He lets me go with a last shove before he steps back and turns to the now horrified girl hiding in Gavin's chest. I let out a breath and straighten my clothing, keeping my eye on the girl. She looks worse than I thought. The brace around her ankle works as a splint and immobilizes her.

"I need you to keep her with you," Josh says as he grabs the bag from Gavin.

"Josh, come on, man. Why? Is this Dylan? The eighteen-year-old who came up here from Texas? Is this why you ran out so fast? What the fuck is happening?"

He pushes past me without saying a word. My mouth drops. I feel like I'm being invaded. I look at Gavin as he helps Dylan into my house. My heart starts racing, and not in a good way. I don't like not knowing things. It's probably why I fit so damn well in this family. None of us like having things go on with no information.

"Once you learn what happened, trust me. You'll understand the reason for this." As soon as Gavin gets her inside, I close the door. Gavin, like Josh, says nothing more. He lifts who I assume is Dylan in his arms and carries her upstairs.

"What the fuck is happening?" I ask myself as I collapse on my couch. I lay down and drop my hands over my face. I rub my eyes with a groan. I hear Josh and Gavin walking down my stairs. They both take seats, but I don't open my eyes. "I'm tired. I've been awake for fucking fifty-three hours. What's going on?"

"Dylan just got thrust into our fucking disaster. That's what's going on," Josh grumbles.

I shake my head because I can't do anything else. "That sounds fairly on par with every other fucking thing happening."

"We wondered where Ethan disappeared to. Now we know," Gavin says.

That gets me to open my eyes and sit up. "Please tell me he's not involved with this shit."

"Can't confirm he's involved with the riot or framing you," Josh begins, "but I can confirm he's here and after Dylan because Dylan identified him."

I look at him, stunned. "The fuck did you just say?"

"Yep. I had a hunch. I had Alec pull the pic of the rogue VV member since it's confirmed he's Ethan. When we found Dylan, she said she was being chased by two people. We showed her the pic of him. She confirmed he was one."

I lean back and close my eyes as I slap my hands against my eyes and rub them. "What the hell is going on?" I murmur to myself. I'm one of the best cops I know, and nothing running through my head that makes all of this make sense is anything good. "So, what happened with her? Why drop her here?" I open my eyes and watch them look at each other.

It's Josh who answers me. "She called Colton in Texas. She wanted Xavier, but he wasn't answering. Colton answered, and Dylan told him there was a riot going on in the city, and she was trying to get to school. She took a Lyft, but noticed she was being followed. She asked the driver to drop her as close to the door to the administration building as he could. He did. The second she got out of the car, she noticed the two guys in the car following her were getting out of theirs with their eyes on her. She ran right through some bushes, tripped, got all scratched up."

"She was on the phone with Colton this entire time. He heard it all. As she was running and confirmed they were chasing her, Xavier, who Colton had gotten out of the shower, called Josh. Dylan got hurt, but she ran anyway."

"Right to the administration office. She found an empty office. The Lyft driver helped her. She locked the door and stayed on the phone. He stayed outside the door the whole time after he got away from Ethan and whoever the fuck he had with him." Josh lets out a low rumble of a growl.

I look between the two of them for a few moments before speaking. "So, you're thinking he's after her. Why?"

"Don't know that yet. We just know it's him." Josh rubs his eyes before laying them on me again. "She stays with you."

I shake my head. "Why not with Rosie? They're friends, right? Or Dallas? She'd be better off with Lance and Damon or you then here with me."

Josh shakes his head as Gavin stands. "No. She stays with you. With you on administrative leave, you can't be out. You can't be seen doing police duties. You're stuck. She's safer with you given you'll be around. I might need to take off."

"Fuck. Josh, she's on the compound. She's as safe as she can possibly be. It doesn't matter who she's with. I'm dealing with enough shit. I don't want to take on the responsibility of bodyguard."

"They know she's with us, man," Gavin says. "They had to have been watching. They know who has her. We need to keep her as isolated as we can in order to protect everyone else."

Suddenly, I figure it out. "Motherfucker. You want to put us both in a safehouse."

Josh grins and pats my knee. "There you go." He stands. "Be ready to go in two hours. I have to make sure the house is set up."

I look at him. "We can't go to the one you kept Aero at. It's compromised."

"It's not. They don't know where it is. Maybe just the area it might be in, but that's not where you're going."

"Fuck, Josh. I'm on administrative leave. I can't leave the city limits, and I need to inform the department where I'm going to fucking be!"

He turns back to me as Gavin opens the door and steps out. "Do you honestly think I don't know that? Be ready, Cole." He glances up the stairs. "Both of you."

He closes my door, and I growl as I stand. I walk angrily up the stairs to my bedroom. A door to one of the three guest bedrooms I have is open. I always keep them closed. I hear quiet crying coming from inside, but there's nothing that's going to get me to step foot in that room. I'm not in any position, nor do I have the goddamn desire, to play protector.

The only reason I'm going along with any of this is for the family. I know with me here, it causes danger to them. If putting me in the penthouse, which is the only logical place Josh can put me, is what needs to be done to protect them, I'll do it.

The only problems?

I won't be alone…

…and there's only one fucking bedroom…

Chapter Three

☙ Dylan ☙

I've never met the cop that lives here, but I know his name is Cole Westwood. I know he works for the police department and was framed for a murder he didn't commit. Josh and Gavin filled me in on all of that on the way here. Other than that, I know nothing about him. Nothing more than he's someone who works with Josh. He's family to them. Which means I can trust him.

I also know he's by far the sexiest man I've ever seen. He's the definition of tall, dark, and handsome, and his amber eyes have the power to cut through a person's soul.

"I'm sure you heard," a baritone, growly voice cuts into my very close to impure thoughts. I jump and wipe my eyes furiously, but refuse to look in his direction. "We're leaving in ten minutes."

I nod and force myself to turn and acknowledge him, but he's already gone. I blink a few times and wonder if I imagined it all. I let out a breath and hobble my way out of the bedroom. He's not in any of the rooms up here, so I make my way to the stairs.

I clear my throat. "Mr. Westwood?"

A few moments later, he appears in all of his overly sexy glory and a scowl on his handsome face. "It's just Cole. For fuck's sake don't go around calling me Mr. Westwood," he growls.

My eyes widen and I shrink a little. "S-sorry. I-I just… uh… d-don't know what I'm s-supposed to bring."

He blinks and stares holes through me. It takes him a few moments to even answer, but by the time he does, I feel like a complete moron. "They didn't bring a lot in here with them. I'd suggest bringing it all, don't you think?" He turns away before I have a chance to respond.

I put my head down, feeling foolish. I didn't know why all of my stuff was brought up here if we were expected to leave right away anyway, but it's probably because Josh thought I might want to clean up. I'm a complete mess. I'm scratched from the bush I ran through. My shirt is torn. My hair is a mess. I've been crying. The only two things I have going for me are I'm alive and my ankle is numb. The jury is still out on if either of them are good things or not, though.

I make sure my phone is tucked in my back pocket, then pick up my bags. They're both big, but I'm used to carrying around a lot of things when I go to cheer competitions. I can handle this.

I sling them over my shoulder, but the extra weight makes walking on my ankle impossible. I whimper but show no weakness. I'm not conditioned that way. I'm the leader. I'm the one who's helping others grow and succeed. I don't fail. I'll never fall under the pressure.

I take a deep breath and limp slowly from the bedroom. I close the door behind me since that's how the other doors up here are. I didn't touch anything in the bedroom. I even straightened the pristine, white blanket on the bed when I got up.

As soon as I reach the stairs, it's glaringly obvious I need help, but I'll never ask for it. Not from Cole, at least. Not from anyone if it means showing a flaw or weakness. I hiss between my teeth and fight back instant tears when I hit the first stair. I adjust the weight and grip the banister with both hands, using it to take some of the weight and support myself as I make my way down.

I ignore the knock on the door as I focus on my task. Getting down the stairs. I see Cole's tensed back heading for the door and opening it. Another person I've never met is standing on the other side. Cole follows him outside with his bags and leaves the door open. No one pays any attention to me, and I'm okay with that. I don't care for anyone to see the pain I'm going through; how much I'm fighting it.

By the time I'm halfway down, I know I'm not getting any further, but I'm too stubborn to give up. Leaning against the railing, sweating from the effort, I drop the bags carefully. My laptop is one of them. I lean down the best I can and gently push them so they slide down the stairs. Cole chooses that moment to walk back into the house.

He shoots me a glare and focuses on my foot. He rolls his eyes and sighs as he strides across the room. He takes the stairs two at a time until he reaches me. I'm shaking with the energy it's taking me to get down the rest of the stairs, but I refuse to let him see that.

"I'm fine."

His amber eyes look like they're on fire when they meet my hazel ones. "I'm not waiting all day for you to prove a point about how tough you are. You can either let me help, or I'll just carry you down. Pick."

I glare at his tone and hold the banister tighter. "I said I got it. I don't need help. I'm already an obvious burden to you."

"You're a burden to us all. Not just me. We have a lot more important shit to deal with than whatever you've managed to get yourself into you."

I scoff and start making my way the rest of the way down the stairs. Every step I take makes me feel like every muscle in both of my legs are being attacked by mini swords of fire. "I said I'll make it."

Cole sighs, but it sounds more like a rumble. The next thing I know, I'm being swung into his arms and carried down the stairs. He sets me down near the couch. I stare at him in shock as he walks back and grabs the bags that landed softly on the floor at the bottom of the stairs.

"Laptop and phone." He picks up the bags and carries them to where I am. He sets them on the arm of the couch. "Any other electronic device. Tablet. Reading device. Take them out."

"What…?"

"You heard me."

My mouth drops a little. "I… my…" I shake my head, trying to clear it. "Why?"

"Because they can be tracked. They need to be checked. Your phone especially."

"But school! How am I supposed to communicate with my advisor and get emails that I need? What about -"

"Fuck, Dylan! Stop arguing and just do what I say!" he barks as he points to the bags.

I jump into action because I don't like being yelled at. My father does it to me and gives me no choice but to obey. I hurry to do what Cole says because I don't know what his consequences for disobedience are. With shaky hands, I accidentally drop my tablet on the floor at Cole's feet. I bend to pick it up quickly and drop it again.

"I -" I hold my hands together to keep them from trembling.

"Fucking hell." He picks it up. "Laptop."

With just as much clumsy speed, I manage to get the laptop out without dropping it. I find my eReader and give it to him before thrusting my cracked phone at him. "Th-that's everything." I expect him to look through my bags just to make sure I'm not lying, but he doesn't. Instead, he shifts everything to one hand and picks up both duffel bags with the other after he zips them with one hand. He points to the door without saying another word.

As quickly as I can, I hobble to the door. He closes it behind us and stays behind me the entire time. I don't know if I'm imagining it, or if the low growls I hear are really coming from him, but they sound dangerous and angry.

I open the back door of the truck in front of me and start to climb in. It's higher than the SUV I came here in, though, and it's not easy. Cole growls low in his throat again, making me jump. His hand grips my waist, and he gently pulls me back. His touch sends lightning all through my body. I hug myself tight because I don't know what to make of that. It's never happened before.

He leans in and puts the bags on the seat. He pushes them across. What I'm sure are his are on the floor. He steps around me and puts my laptop, reader, tablet, and phone on the front seat before he's back at my side.

"Can you get in? Or do you need help?"

I look down because I don't want to admit that I can't get in on my own without hurting myself even more. "I'm not sure if it's broken," I whisper.

He sighs and bends. As he had on the stairs, he lifts me in his arms with an ease that makes my heart beat faster. He sets me on the seat and closes the door behind me. He quickly gets in the front seat.

"Here's her electronics," he says to the man next to him.

"Lance will take care of them."

"She has school shit."

"I said, Lance would deal with it, Cole." The man backs out of the driveway and starts driving down the private road in the Crane and Lucinio compound. A few moments later, he pulls over, and a tall man with light-brown hair hurries out of the house. I haven't seen him in a while, but I recognize him as Lance.

"Got her stuff?" Lance asks.

Cole hands it to him. "Get it back quick. She needs it, and I don't want to be fucking annoyed the whole damn time."

Lance rolls his eyes as he takes it. He looks back at me. "He's usually a pretty good guy. Don't take any shit from him."

I don't get to say anything before Cole's window is going up. I bite my lip and wave instead. "I wish I could see Rosie, at least," I say quietly.

"No time," Cole says.

"Shut up, Westwood," the driver says. "You're not the only one having a bad fucking day." He pulls away from the curb and glances back at me. "I'm Dane Michaels. This asshole's Lieutenant. Lance is right. He's usually pretty good. Don't take his shit."

Cole grumbles and shakes his head as he leans it against the window. I don't say anything. I just nod and settle in for what I hope isn't a long ride. I just want to hide. I don't want to talk to Cole. I don't want to talk to anyone but Rosie and Dallas, and I can't even do that. It's like I'm home in Texas all over again. Alone and isolated.

Several attempts at fighting tears and pain later, we arrive at a very tall building along the lake in the city. I hadn't noticed, but there's a black SUV in front and behind us. There are two men in dark suits that step out of both of them. They both look around before approaching our truck. If I didn't know how Josh Lucinio worked, I'd be freaked out, but I know these are guards.

No thanks to Cole, the sexy prick.

One of the guards opens my door and holds out a hand. "Can I help you down?"

"Yes, please," I say quietly, taking his hand. He helps me down. Another guard leads me inside. "Oh. Um… my stuff is still in there."

"Don't worry about your stuff, ma'am. It'll be brought up. We need to get you to safety." He stops at a desk with two guards. "Mr. Westwood and Ms. Remington have arrived."

"We'll have a guard come up after they're settled to get Ms. Remington checked into the system. Mr. Westwood is good to go," one of the guards behind the desk says. He's a little older.

The guard I'm with nods his respect and helps me to a set of elevators. He positions me near the wall and glances towards the lobby we were just in. A few moments later, Cole storms in with his bags slung over his shoulder. Dane has mine. The other three guards don't follow.

Once we all step into the elevator, the ride up is silent. As the doors open, Cole glances at me and hangs back as the guard escorts me out. He runs a card and scans his hand at a door. When the panel turns green, he opens the door and guides me inside to the largest penthouse I've ever seen, and I come from a well to do family.

I stop in the center of the living room and just look around. The floor to ceiling windows overlook the lake and a few other buildings. There's a giant TV above a large fireplace. The furniture, brown in color, looks to be made with the most comfortable fabric.

The penthouse is an open-floor plan. There's a large kitchen and game room with a pool table. Down the hall, there are a couple of doors. I don't know what's behind them, but I'm excited to explore and find out. Down the other hall, on the opposite end of the living room, is one door. Outside the game room is a large jacuzzi. The only thing missing is a pool, but I don't even miss it because the view is fantastic. I've already picked out my own place to curl up and read.

"There's only one bedroom," Cole rumbles behind me.

I turn to look at him and see everyone else is already gone. "Oh." I take a deep breath and turn away quickly.

"I'm too tall for the couches, so you have two choices. I'll arrange the couches so they go together and create a bed for you. Or you sleep in the bed with me."

I whip my head to him in disbelief. I'm about to let out a squeak of a reply, but I see the smirk on his face, and I'm suddenly infuriated. "Fuck you. Honestly. I'll take the couches. I don't need your fucking help."

"Tsk, tsk. Such a mouth on you, princess."

I hobble towards the couch, seething. "Don't call me princess." I hate being called princess. Everyone in my school called me that just because I lived a privileged life as a Senator's daughter. Every time I hear it now, it makes me want to punch the person who said it in the mouth.

"Bathroom with another shower is down the hall across from the game room. There's also a gym down there. Towels and shit is in the closet in the bathroom. Make yourself at home. We'll be here a while, princess."

I let out my own low growl at the stupid pet name but say nothing to him. He takes the hint and takes his stuff to the bedroom. Refusing to allow him to help me at all, I start moving things. The couches are across from each other. They look like they fit together, so maybe they're meant to go together and create a large bed or something.

In order to get them together, though, I'll have to move a couple of coffee tables. And since it would be weird for me to sleep with one back of the couch at the window and the other towards the door, I have to move them so they're vertical.

After moving the table, I set to work on the couches, but by the time I get them moved so they're facing the way that I want them to, I'm so sore that tears are streaming down my face. My body feels like it's on fire. I wipe the sweat from my head and tears from my eyes as I turn and grab my bags. I drag them to the bathroom with me because I'm too weak and worn out to carry them.

Once I get to the bathroom, I see there's only a shower, toilet, and sink. Though it's decent sized and the shower looks like it has a massager, I was hoping for a bath. Having no other choice but to settle for the shower, I start undressing, hissing at the sting of the scratches. I'm terrified to take the brace Gavin put on my foot off. It feels really swollen, but Josh did have a doctor look at it. He said there's no break, but I'm not totally certain about that.

I wince after getting it off. I was right. It's got an ugly bruise and looks like it's the size of a softball. I close my eyes for a moment to gain my strength and bearings about me before stepping in the shower. I don't know how long I stand under the hot spray before I finally clean up and get out, but I feel a lot more relaxed. All I want is to go to bed.

I resign myself to not being able to sleep in what I felt would be a pretty nice bed, but the couch was comfortable when I tested it out earlier.

It will do for tonight. I can work more at the bed and trying to figure out how to fit it together tomorrow. Maybe a good night's sleep will do me good.

Hell, maybe it will do Cole good, too. Everyone has said he's a good guy usually. Maybe he's just stressed out and tired. Perhaps by tomorrow he'll feel better. Hopefully, we both will. I have a lot of phone calls to make, and I'm hoping he'll let me use his phone. I'm sure my cousins are beside themselves with worry having not heard from me. And I can't imagine how Dallas and Rosie are feeling. If they're anything like me, and they are, they're probably waiting for a check in at the very least, and to see me at the most.

Once I finish drying off and brushing out my dark hair, I find a tank top and shorts to sleep in. I grab a hoodie just in case I get cold. I change, being careful of my ankle, and then drag my stuff back out to the living room. I'm not sure if I should let my ankle be tonight or if I should put the brace back on. I've never had a sprain before. I've never had a broken bone or been really injured either.

Then again, I've also never been chased and put into protective custody with a man who is both the hottest and biggest jerk in the world.

I shake thoughts of everything out of my head as I reach the living room. I drop my stuff next to the chair and stop dead in my tracks. To my surprise, the couch is put together like a bed. There's a sheet that looks so soft underneath a light blanket and a comforter that I can't wait to sink down under. The blankets are turned down, like at a hotel when a person asks for turn down service.

I glance at the bedroom in disbelief. I didn't think Cole would do something like this for me. I very obviously rub him the wrong way. I decided that in the shower. I make my way to the bed and see two braces with notes.

Next to one that seems to have more padding, the note simply says, *Daytime.* Next to one that looks like an ankle sock, the note says, *Wear this tonight. It will stabilize your ankle so you don't fuck something up in your sleep.*

I glance at the room again before putting both notes with the daytime ankle brace on the end table next to the couch. I'm met with another surprise note next to a glass of water and a pill. *Drink all of the water. I mean it. The pill is a narcotic prescribed by Dr. Freeman for the pain to help you sleep. It'll knock your ass out. You'll need the water to combat feeling like you have a hangover in the morning.*

"What the hell is happening?" I whisper. "Why is he suddenly being so nice?"

I take the pills and down half the water. He even thought to add ice cubes to it. It's a tall glass. I intend to drink the rest once I get the stabilizer on, but once I'm settled, I'm already too tired to reach for it.

Seconds after my head hits the pillow, I'm in la la land with no chance of moving until my exhausted body lets me.

Chapter Four

☙ Cole ☙

The next morning, an entire sixteen hours after I went to sleep, I grumble as I watch the news in the bedroom. My family and Chicago PD are dominating it. Even national news is reporting that the mafia owns the police department and they're protecting one of their own. On both sides of the line. Carmella works for the local news station and is playing right into the rhetoric that's obviously wanted. Everyone they've talked to hates me and the Lucinio and Crane families more than anything in the world.

I rub a hand down my face and groan. So much for Ryan's and Josh's control over the media. They're not reporting what they would want them to right now. That's not going to get them the views. There's no way this is getting shoved under the rug until the investigation is complete.

That's not happening anytime soon. I know how long investigations take. The department isn't going to want anyone to know they're working with the mafia to clear a dirty cop. It's not just the murder I'm going down for. It's now being reported that I'm a drug dealer and somehow involved in the illegal gambling and drug trafficking ring. One of the national outlets even said I work with the cartel and that the mafia is after me because of it.

Everything is outlandish and so out of control that I feel out of control myself. I don't like that. I don't like feeling as if I don't have a handle on anything, especially my fucking life. The truth is, I don't even have control over that. My life lies in the hands of my family and the fucking police department. I can't even be near the investigation because if I touch it, it's easily turned into some kind of corruption scheme. Not like I'm not already facing enough of that accusation.

"Fuck my entire life twelve times over," I growl as I shut the TV off. "Maybe I'll fucking ban TV in the penthouse. No news. No newspapers. No TV." I tug a pair of gray sweats on with the intention of working out, but my stomach growls instead.

Foregoing a shirt, I grab my phone and stride out to the kitchen. I wouldn't have bothered with the phone at all, but if Josh or Dane or anyone needs me, this is currently my lifeline.

I make a beeline for the coffee and immediately start brewing a cup before I even attempt starting breakfast. Coffee is lifeblood to me. I can't function without it, so while it brews, I start pulling things out for breakfast. I'm in the mood to splurge, so I take bacon, hashbrowns, eggs, butter, and wheat bread out. Deciding a skillet is necessary, I go back to the fridge for tomatoes, onions, and peppers. I'm thankful everything I need is here, but I'll have to go through and see if I'm missing anything. If I'm going to be here a while, I'm not going without my favorites.

Once my coffee is done, I take a long drink of it not carrying at all that it's hot enough to scald me. My tongue, however, isn't on the same page. The moment the liquid hits it, I instantly feel my mistake.

"Fuck," I growl low and take a more cautious sip, glaring at the offending steam coming from my cup. Once some of the morning magic hits my tastebuds, I'm in a much better mood. Though, since it was in the fucking ditch to begin with, it's still not great.

I set down the cup and start putting the bacon in the pan. I start that and then start cutting the tomatoes, onions, and peppers. I throw them in a pan to cook and flip the bacon.

"Mmm…"

I freeze at the groan of pain coming from behind me. I almost managed to forget about her. Dylan Remington. The sexy brunette with fuck me, golden hazel eyes, a smile I'd die for, and a body I'd get down on my knees and beg to worship.

And way too fucking young for me. I'm thirty-six. She's eighteen.

I look over my shoulder when she whimpers. She's trying to sit up, but one of her hands is over her eyes. I look at the water glass on the end table next to her and chuckle when I see it's only half gone. I warned her, so I don't feel bad that she feels like she's been hit by a truck.

"Oh God," she murmurs. She makes it halfway up, but the rest of the way is probably going to make her puke. I shake my head and turn back to breakfast.

Last night, after she went to the shower, I came out here because I took pity on her. I could hear her moving shit around out here. I knew she was struggling, but she very clearly stated she didn't want help. I almost came out here several times to help her, but I wasn't in the mood for her smart mouth. I was tired as hell and just as irritable. So, when she gave up and went to the shower, I made my way out here and finished what she couldn't.

Not that she didn't get pretty far. I was impressed at her progress. As I was finishing it, one of our guards showed up and gave me the pills Dr. Freeman prescribed along with the two braces for her ankle. As soon as I saw the name of the prescription, I knew what the results for her would be. Percocet is basically Oxycodone with Tylenol added to it. It's strong enough to knock me on my ass, and she's half my size. Being I'm a cop, I also know how addictive it is. No way is she getting it during the day. She'll not only feel high, but she's far more likely to get addicted.

I also know how people feel in the morning after taking it. I wanted to prevent it, and the best way to do that is a full glass of water. Doing some kind of sugary sports drink does nothing but make a person feel sick. Not that something like that happens to everyone. Some people, it simply has no effect. Until I knew how she'd react to it, though, I didn't want her touching it. The directions are to take one, but I think even that's too much for her.

"I'm dying."

I chuckle. "You should've drank the water."

"It wouldn't have helped. I feel like I'm going to lose the contents of my stomach. And since there's nothing in it, that's going to be bad."

"If you would've drank the water like I told you to, you'd feel a lot better."

"What did you give me?"

"Percocet. Doc checked your medical history. You've had it once before. Which was surprising. They don't usually give that to kids under twelve."

She's quiet. She's probably thinking the same thoughts I was. Finally, she sighs. "When would I possibly have been given that? I've never had that severe of an injury. I twisted my knee once when I was younger, but I don't really remember it being that severe to be prescribed something that strong."

I put hashbrowns into the pan the vegetables are in. "You never should've been. I have Lance looking into it, but I think you were poisoned or some shit. Kids shouldn't have that."

"You're accusing my parents of poisoning me? Why?"

"I'm not accusing anyone of anything. I'm giving you a theory that's been bothering me. There's no other reason you should've had that unless it was meant to make you sick or high enough to not remember something. Percocet could kill a child if not dosed correctly."

"What makes you think it wasn't dosed correctly?"

I glare at the ceiling and shake my head as I start taking the done bacon out of the pan and putting it on a paper towel to soak up the excess fat. "Because I trust our doctor, Dylan. And because I've been around a lot longer than you. The dosage you were given is the same as they'd give a grown man or woman. And because a child should never be given a narcotic like that without being under doctor supervision. You weren't. And before you argue, I fucking know because your chart doesn't mention a hospital stay." I set the pan aside and grab a smaller one for the eggs I scrambled.

"Look, Cole. I don't know what impression you have of me or my family, but I can assure you they weren't trying to kill me or make me sick. I think I'd remember."

"Sure. Yeah. I'm sure you would," I say as sarcastically as possible. "Get up. You'll feel better after you eat."

"Highly doubtful. I'll pass, thanks."

"That wasn't a request or an option. I said get up. You need to eat."

"Last I checked, I'm an adult. Fully grown woman capable of making my own decisions. Contrary to popular belief, I'm pretty smart and managed to get into a top ten university all by myself."

I chuckle, though it's anything but bright and chipper. She has no idea, but she's just challenged a side of me I'm not sure she wants to see. A side that's been buried for a long time. No woman I've ever come across has ever come close to awakening him from his slumber, but fuck if this woman, of all of the women I've been with, didn't do just that.

My stomach tightens. My dick hardens. My muscles coil and tense. I don't even bother holding him down because there's no point. I love a fucking challenge just as much as any man. I don't turn around, though. I do nothing more than cover the pan of eggs with a lid as I shut the head off. I toss the hashbrowns and pop some toast into the toaster. Only then do I turn.

I lean against the counter and fold my arms over my chest. "For someone who claims to be so smart and an adult, princess, you're acting pretty stupid."

"Good thing I didn't ask for your opinion."

"Good thing I wasn't giving you one. It's facts. Allowing yourself to continue with the effects of the pain pill as you are is going to make you sick to your stomach. I give you fifteen minutes before you're stumbling to the bathroom and puking. You're small. You can't possibly weigh more than one-twenty. You're athletic and think nothing can touch you, but I can assure you. You took that pill on an empty stomach. Leaving it that way will force the bile up your throat and out your mouth. You'll have a headache the entire day. And if you take another one tonight, you won't be able to hold it down. You'll throw it up within twenty minutes because there's nothing in your stomach to help you. Eating will combat the effects of what you're feeling. It's like alcohol. You need the nourishment to soak it up and allow it to work its best."

"Doesn't it say something about take with or without food? Isn't that what most pain pills say? Shouldn't I be following that?"

"Yes. But do you really want to risk all of that when you could just listen to someone older and wiser who actually has a fucking doctor behind him giving him this information, or has maybe been through it himself?"

She glares at me. When I don't make any motion to turn away, she throws a mini tantrum that's adorable as fuck and throws her covers off. The first thing I see is the hoodie she's wearing that covers up her curves. Disappointing.

The second makes my breath catch. If I could spin around so I don't see it, I would, but I'm frozen to the ground. The shorts she's wearing are very short and must've moved on her while she was sleeping because I can very clearly see she's not wearing any panties. Her pussy is bare and causes my dick to react in a way that would embarrass me if I was paying any attention at all to it.

She stands up slowly and lets out a breath as she starts walking towards the counter. I thank whoever might hear me that I get my wits back before she sees the impressive tent in my sweats. I quickly turn away and close my eyes.

"Obviously, I'm not winning this, but I still think you're exaggerating."

I swallow. Hard. I start thinking of anything I can that's unsexy just to get my cock to go back down to a reasonable size that I can at least try to hide. I know my size. It's not easy to keep it hidden, but I can handle it a lot better when it's not sticking straight out like a fucking flagpole.

"I'm not exaggerating the possibilities of what can happen. I'd prefer to avoid it. That's all." The toast pops up, and I take it out to start buttering it.

She clears her throat. "Um... I'll just take toast, please. And the bacon and eggs."

"The hashbrowns -"

"Have onions in them."

"So?"

"I can't eat them."

"Why? Don't like them? Because there are a lot of benefits -"

"I'm allergic, Cole."

I stop what I'm doing and start looking to see if anything I've touched could have been contaminated with onions and make a mental note to have them thrown out. I washed my hands after cutting them. The knife is in the sink. I didn't put the eggs near the onions. I didn't use the same spatula. I try my best not to panic and scrap everything I've cooked, but it's not the easiest.

Satisfied that I'm not going to kill her unintentionally, and after washing my hands again just to be sure, I put her toast, some bacon, and the eggs on a plate for her. "What else are you allergic to? I'll get rid of it."

She smiles softly. "Nothing. Just onions. My throat starts hurting a little, but if I take Benadryl, I'm okay. I don't need an Epipen or anything. If I touch them, I break out."

I silently breathe a sigh of relief and nod as I dish up my own food. I take my phone out and text the guards at the desk about onions just so this mistake doesn't happen again. I'll clean everything up with disinfectant as soon as we're done with breakfast. In the meantime, I'll be watching her closely.

"I'll get rid of the onion and do the dishes. I'll clean up after. You stay out of the kitchen. Understand?"

Her eyes widen a little at my tone. A dominant tone that I can't help using with her. I have no control. It comes far too naturally. She looks down at her plate. "Okay."

We both eat in silence. When we're finished, I make good on my promise and clean up while she disappears. She didn't seem to have any symptoms of an allergic reaction, so I feel good about letting her out of my sight. As soon as I'm done, I leave her a note that says to write down what she wants for food and drinks and everything for her personal needs.

I make my way to the gym and start my workout. I need it to burn off the pent up feelings I already have as well as everything she's made me feel since the second I saw her. She's gorgeous. There's no denying it, but I'm twice her age and nothing close to what she deserves.

It doesn't stop me from wanting to unravel the mystery that is her, though. She's different from other rich as hell girls her age. She's a lot more like Rosie and Dallas in that she knows she has money, but doesn't care or flaunt it. She still works hard to achieve her dreams. It's obvious in how proud she is to be going to Kingston University. She's proud of all of her accomplishments because she's done them on her own.

Makes me wonder how much of daddy's money was really used to help her out along the way, but she doesn't strike me as the type who leans on it. Maybe for college, but who doesn't need their parents for that? It's how the government gets so much more money. Less grants given means more in their pockets.

Growling at my cynicism, I put extra work into my lifting until I'm breaking a sweat. I move onto a different set of lifts and try to shove the beautiful girl out of my head. Everything I'm thinking is inappropriate. Especially how fucking sexy the peek of her I got was.

I'm sure she's scared as hell about what's going on in her own life. Add in that her bodyguard is a man currently being accused as a murderer, and her life has to be just as upside down as mine is.

There's nothing about our situation that's good. Our only hope right now is relying on my family to get us out of it.

And while they're doing that, she cannot be my downfall, no matter how much I want her in my bed. I'm used to one-night stands just as I am to having a girlfriend for a couple of months. Carmella was the longest relationship I've had in a long time, but it was purely physical.

I could fall for a girl like Dylan.

And falling is something I'm never doing again…

Chapter Five

☙ Dylan ☙

I lean back and give up on trying to get my foot elevated at a comfortable level. I've tried using pillows, but it's not high enough. The couch cushions are too high. I tried lying down and using the back of the couch to elevate it, but it's too hard for the back of my leg, and I couldn't get the stupid ice pack to stay in place.

I'm hot. I don't know where the thermostat is to adjust the temperature, and the sun seems to be beating right on the window and beaming at me, even though it's not even on the same side of the building the window is. I'm not wearing a lot of clothing. I'm just wearing jean shorts and a tank top. I put my hair up into a messy bun. It's still way too hot.

I gave up a long time ago in finding a comfortable position to be in. So instead, I'm on my back like a starfish on the bed. Maybe if I stay like this, I'll just melt into water and disappear. Maybe I can somehow manifest myself at Kingston University in my dorm where none of anything that's happened would have.

That isn't totally true. Cole might be a complete jerk, but I can see underneath the tough exterior. He's got a caring side. He's protective. And there's another side to him that I don't quite understand. Something that calls to me. Something dangerous and dark, but I'm not afraid of it. I just want to explore every part of him.

Not to mention, he's hot. He's the sexiest man I've ever seen. He has to be like six-feet-four. His amber eyes light me on fire every time I catch them. He's muscular. He's built like he knows his way around the gym just as well as I'm sure he knows his way around the bedroom. And oh, to be one of those conquests. I'm sure he has had many, but I wouldn't be upset being one of them. I bet he could erase the memory of my one and only sexual encounter.

Prom night in the back of a pick-up truck. I'd been with the guy for a couple of years. He was a basketball player, though far from one of the stars of the team. My cousins weren't too fond of him, but they didn't really say much about him either. I took that as my okay to date him. Little did I know that the day after we had the worst sex imaginable, he'd break up with me. It was my first time, but I knew it wasn't his. Given that he was more experienced, I thought he'd guide me so I knew what he liked. I definitely wasn't correct in that assumption.

I doubt Cole is the kind of man who would do that. I bet he'd be very attentive and take the lead I'd need him to. He doesn't seem like the relationship type, but I'm not sure that would matter.

I sigh. Who am I kidding? It would matter. I'm not a one and done kind of woman. It's probably my biggest downfall. I trust too fast and fall too hard. My cousins were right to always be the ones protecting me. It wasn't for them or their egos. It was for me and my safety. I don't know what I was thinking coming to Chicago and being away from them. It was stupid. I've only been here a couple of days and I'm already in trouble. I'm such a disappointment.

I open my eyes when I hear the refrigerator door open. Cole is still in those stupid gray sweats that leave nothing to the imagination. He's big. I can see the outline of his dick very clearly. It makes it hard to think. He makes it hard for my mind to be on anything other than him. He's cut. His abs are to die for. He doesn't have hair on his chest. He has one tattoo. Angel wings on his back with a number underneath them. *10842*. I don't know what it means, but I'm curious to know the significance to him.

"Is there a pool here? I really need to cool off."

"No. Take a cold bath." Cole stands to his full height with a bottle of water in his hand. He opens the lid as he turns to me and leans against the counter. I can see the droplets of sweat beading from his skin.

I avert my eyes and suck in a breath that I hope is quiet. "Can you put on a shirt or something?"

He rumbles low and takes a drink of his water. I feel his eyes burning a hole in me. "Why? Am I distracting?"

So much. Words I want to say but refuse to. Also words I'd never be able to. He's very much out of my league, and I really need to get vision of him naked out of my thoughts. It's not who I am. I'm not a slut.

"No." I force my gaze up. "But you just worked out, and you're sweating. You're getting it all over the place."

He studies me like I'm a science experiment until I'm shivering under his gaze and hugging myself. I sit up and try to do anything else. I start messing with pillows again, trying to make them comfortable for my foot. I haven't put the other brace on for the day because I don't know how. It's like a compression sock or something, and my foot is too swollen to get it on.

He says nothing more to me as he walks to his room. By the time he comes out wearing shorts and a t-shirt, I'm not faring any better. I'm close to crying because my foot hurts and the ice pack is still refreezing. I can't get my foot at the right elevation, and I'm hot.

"What the fuck are you even trying to do?" he asks.

Fed up completely with everything, I pick up a pillow and throw it at him as hard as I possibly can before bursting into tears. He catches it and glares at me, but before he can say a word, words spew from my mouth like word vomit.

"I'm supposed to be enjoying independence right now in my own college dorm room! Instead, I'm here in a penthouse with a guy who hates my very existence as much as he hates life. I'm being chased by a biker gang I have nothing to do with." Suddenly feeling hysterical, I throw another pillow at him. He catches that one, too, but I continue before he can open his mouth. "I can't even tell my friends and family that I'm okay because I don't have my phone! I can't contact the school to reschedule my meeting! I'm going to miss tryouts for the only thing I'm good at! I can't go through and pick my potential classes because I don't have my laptop! I can't read because I didn't think to pack any physical book until I was settled in my dorm and went home to get the rest of my stuff!"

"Jesus."

"I'm hot! It feels like it's a hundred degrees in here! There's no pool! I don't have a bathtub in the bathroom I'm using, so I can't take a cold bath! I can't take a cold shower because I can't stand on my stupid fucked up foot! I can't make it comfortable enough when I elevate it so it doesn't hurt! The ice pack is still refreezing! Happy now?" I wipe my eyes, completely embarrassed. I turn away from him and burrow into the very messed up couch. I've been tossing and turning so much that it looks like a hurricane hit it. "Go ahead. Think I'm crazy. I'm just a spoiled princess. I don't care. Everyone else does."

A few moments later, I feel him sit behind me. I don't turn towards him. I don't lose control like that. I can't remember the last time I cried. Crying was always a sign of weakness. I couldn't show that kind of emotion as a Senator's daughter. I always had to be perfect. A robot. I knew my role then and know it just as well now.

"What I'm dealing with isn't your fault. I'm fucking bitter. I feel like I got hit by a train that kept going, and I'm just hanging on for life. I was blindsided by everything. I'm being considered a murderer. I'm on leave from the only thing that kept me even slightly sane waiting for an investigation to be completed that shouldn't even be happening. My entire life is hanging in the balance here. And before you say anything, I get it. I know yours was just as much fucked over and upturned. You don't need my bullshit, which is why I was telling Josh and Gavin to take you anywhere else. I get the reasons behind it all. I know why Josh made the decision he did, but it's not helpful to either of us right now. Truth is, we're going to have to deal with it because we have no other choice."

His words don't seem to have the calming effect he thinks they do because I'm even more infuriated that everything is happening, and I'm caught in the middle. But being the always good girl I am, I don't let on that I'm upset. Instead, I do what I always do. I put on a smile I don't feel and dry my eyes. Big girls don't cry, right?

"I'll be fine, Cole. I'm sorry. Don't worry about me." I focus on making myself calm, turning off my emotions like I'm so good at doing.

Cole gets up and walks somewhere. I don't know where and don't care. I close my eyes and hear him opening the refrigerator again. A few minutes later, after a lot of rustling, I feel him sit down again. Only this time, he's on the other side of the couch where my feet are.

"These laces are adjustable. It makes it easier to get the brace on. RICE. Rest, ice, compress, elevate. I'm sure you know that."

I open my eyes and look at him, slightly confused. He doesn't make eye contact, but he's adjusting the brace and making it as wide as possible. "I... knew. I guess."

He nods a little as he takes my foot gently in his large hand. He slides the brace on easily, though it's still tight. He gently puts my foot down and adjusts the laces before velcroing the stabilization wings in place.

"Too tight?"

I shake my head, feeling almost immediate relief. "No... Thank you."

"Next is Tylenol." He hands me two gelcaps and a bottle of water. "It will help with the pain while the compression will help with the swelling." He watches me take the tablets with the water. He holds his hand out for the bottle. I put the lid back on and hand it to him. He stands. "Now, we need to fix this bed so you can be comfortable. I'll help you up."

Bewildered, I let him help me out of the bed. I watch him adjust the sheets and blankets. He puts the pillows where they're supposed to be. He leaves the cushions on one side of the couch alone and takes the ones from the other side.

All it takes is a look from him. I crawl back into the bed and settle with my back against the side with the cushions. I'm facing the giant TV and fireplace. Cole lifts my leg and puts cushions on top of each other. Before I can protest about how I've tried that, he puts smaller throw pillows under my thigh and knee so I'm not stressing it by elevating it. I can relax it fully.

I also notice I'm cooling down considerably. "Did... you... turn the air on or something?"

"I turned the temp down. It's central air." He hands me my water back. I take it. "Do you need anything else?"

"Why are you suddenly being so nice?" I look up at his handsome, chiseled face.

He smirks. "I don't know. Maybe you're growing on me." He shrugs. I bite my lip and look down, trying to hide the smile. "Did you write down the stuff you needed like I told you to?"

I nod. "Yes, sir," I almost whisper.

It takes him a moment to respond, but he clears his throat before he does. I glance up at him. Once again, his eyes look like they're about to erupt into an inferno. "Uh... good." He reaches in his pocket as he glances over his shoulder. He looks down at me and hands me his phone. "Give the people you want a call, but your location is top secret. No one knows. Even if Dallas or Rosie ask you how the penthouse is going, you don't confirm or deny you're here."

"W-why?" I furrow my brows.

"Because even though my phone has protections put into place, we don't know if people broke through. It's a less than one percent chance of that ever happening, but that's still a chance I'm not willing to take. There are scramblers in this building, so your location won't be compromised. We also take other precautions with our phones to make sure they're untrackable, but we absolutely can't be sure everything is one-hundred percent. There's no guarantees."

"What do I say if anyone asks about the penthouse?"

"Hang up. No one should know. I know. Guards do. Josh and Gavin do. Dane knows. Anyone who was told where you are was also told not to say it or discuss it. If they do, something's wrong. Hang up and tell me because it means we need to get out. Don't talk about anything that could give away your location. Don't talk about the view. Don't talk about the way the sun looks when it rises. All of that stuff is a clue."

"Okay. Um... can I call my parents and cousins?"

"You can. But same rules."

"Okay."

"I'm going to give this list to the guards and get rid of the stuff that has onions or onion powder in here."

"Oh, um. That stuff on the list... I guess..." I stop myself and shake my head. "Never mind."

He raises an eyebrow as he glances over the list. After a moment, he chuckles. "I assume this was you trying to be sassy to me?"

I blush. "Maybe."

"So, how much of this stuff do you actually need? Bras and panties? Tampons?"

"I do actually need it all. I really didn't know what was happening. I only planned on being here a couple of days. I only have stuff packed for that long and an extra outfit just in case I needed it. If I can't go home like I planned, I guess I... I mean, I probably could've been less... specific."

"I'm not going to make them get you a red negligee or assless chaps. But that might be kinda fun for me."

I blush even darker and hold out my hand, refusing to look at him. "I was messing around. I was mad at you. I'll redo the list. I forgot I put that stuff on there."

He laughs. "I got it. You're gonna have to add sizes, though. I don't think we want to trust my guesses."

If I blush any darker, I'm going to turn into chili pepper or something. "Oh God. I really don't want a strange guy shopping for me."

"Good thing we have good guards. Discreet. Who have wives or girlfriends to help."

I don't know why that makes me feel a little relief. He hands me the list, and I'm internally grateful that he blacked out the parts obviously only meant for him. I have no desire to get assless chaps. I have no use for them or the sexy negligee that I also added *to parade around and drive you crazy in.*

I don't even know what got into me. I was mad at him for being such a jerk and so hot at the same time. I never should've done that. I put things on there meant to embarrass him. I should've known he'd somehow make it as sexy as he is. Short shorts? Tight pants? I'm an idiot.

I add sizes to everything and say specifically the type of tampons I'll need. I feel bad anyone else is going to have to buy me things on this list, especially the tampons. "Maybe I could just order these things."

"No, princess. No deliveries. Security nightmare."

I sigh. "Stop calling me princess."

"Sure thing, princess."

I take a deep breath and close my eyes. "Can you also please get me Landon's number? I want to know how he is."

His eyes narrow, and I wonder if he's jealous. "Crush on the cab driver?"

"Lyft driver. Thank you. There's a difference."

He rolls his eyes, indifference sliding into place like a second skin. "Whatever you want, sweetheart."

And all at once, I'm pissed off again. All thoughts of how stupidly sexy he is crash against the window, and I see red. "Fuck you, Cole."

"Anytime, princess." He strides to the door and disappears, closing it behind him.

"I hate you, Cole Westwood. Fucking hate you."

I start dialing my parents first and push all thoughts of Cole the Asshole out of my mind.

Chapter Six

🍎 Cole 🍎

(One Week Later)

"Come on, Josh. We're both going fucking insane here. She's driving me to the brink of jumping off the balcony."

"Wave to the guards on your way down. The heat isn't off either of you, yet."

I sigh and rub my head. "Then what the hell am I supposed to do about her and tryouts? School? I can't exactly take her to any of that if I'm on house arrest, and she can't be seen in public."

Josh groans. "Look. I know she's pissed. I do. But there's nothing I can do about this. I can take her myself, but tryouts have to be indoors, and the university isn't cooperating with me on that. They do tryouts on the football field. If I bring in the people I need to protect her, Cole, she's under a lot more scrutiny."

"She's under a lot of it anyway. Cheerleading is her life. It's the only thing she has right now that she can control. Telling me she can't enjoy it isn't acceptable. I love you, man. I respect the hell out of you. You know that, but we need to figure this out. She's already had her entire world taken from her. I can handle that being taken from me, but she's only eighteen and doing her best just to fucking function right now. Don't make me tell her I can't even do this for her."

He takes a few moments to answer. "When are tryouts again?"

"The end of June. Two weeks from today."

"I'll do my best, man. I will, but I need to get you cleared first. I don't like our family being apart with Ethan on the loose. It's obvious his goal is to divert my attention so I'm not solely focused on tracking his ass down."

"I'm sure he also knows I'm your tracker. That's why he's focused on me. Take me out, it weakens your ability to find him."

"I don't think he expected you to be released. I think he thought he had us. Cops are targets in prison. I'd bet everything that he believed prison would take care of you."

"I don't doubt that for a second." I turn away from the window in my bedroom that overlooks the city. The bedroom is large. The floor to ceiling windows are on three sides. I can see everything. "What's the status on the pool?"

"That's the other reason I was calling. It's done. She's not going to get much sun because things are enclosed now, but she'll be safe if she needs to get away from you."

I laugh. "She'll be happy to hear that. I'm not the only one who wants to jump off a balcony."

Josh chuckles. "Just give me a few more days. Lance is close, then the department needs to finalize their report for the Superintendent. Realistically, I don't think we're going to be more than two weeks getting you cleared. I think it'll take a week or so, but you know I don't like making promises like that."

"What about the onion issue?"

"Everyone knows. When you get back, the girls will have everything taken care of. No onions around her or for family events."

"Okay. Not like I know she'll stick around, but if she's friends with Rosie and Dallas, I feel like she will."

"Yeah, of course."

I raise an eyebrow because he sounded like he knows something I don't. "That wasn't laced with fucking sarcasm at all."

"Not at all. Just hang tight. I'll talk to you later." Josh hangs up, and I grumble.

"Yeah. Not at all." I shake my head and walk out of the bedroom to the living room. Dylan is sitting on a chair with a sketchbook in her lap. It's been an extension of her since the second the guards brought it. "When are you going to show me those drawings?"

"Never. They're personal. No one sees my drawings."

"Oh, come on. Not parents? Cousins? Friends?"

She stays focused on her drawing. "No one."

"They can't be that bad that you show no one."

She rolls her eyes and glares at me. As usual, I react to her in a way that pisses me off. "I didn't say they were bad. I said they're personal."

"Whatever. Come with me."

"I would rather not. I'm comfortable for the first time all day."

"I wasn't asking."

"And I don't do well with orders."

I clench my fists and shoot her my own glare. If she keeps smarting off, my dick is going to become a lot more prominent in my jeans than it already is. I unclench my fists and walk as calmly as I can towards her. She's a fucking brat, and all I can think of is how badly I want to spank her ass while finger fucking her until she's about to come only to stop and keep her from her sweet release.

When I lean over her chair, she quickly closes her book and looks up at me as she shoves it underneath her. "Cole!"

"Relax. Fuck. I'm not looking. I don't care that much."

Pain crosses her eyes, but she quickly hides it behind the familiar hatred she's grown so accustomed to showing. The truth is, I do care. I'd love to see what she's drawing, but I don't want to get that close to her. She's the kind of girl I could fall in love with. I've been there and done that. Not willing to do it again.

"I don't want to follow you. Go away. Leave me alone."

"No. Let's go."

"I said I don't want to! What part of that can't you get through your thick and stubborn fucking skull! Leave me alone!" she screams.

"Dylan, I'm not fucking around. Either follow, or I fucking make you. Your call." I stand and move to the front of the chair.

"I...! Am...! Not...! Following...! You...! Anywhere!" She stands and tries to push past me, but she's really no match. I grab her around the waist and bend just enough to lift her and throw her over my shoulder. "Ah!" she screams. "Get off me! Put me down!"

She wiggles to get free, but I hold her tighter and swat her perky, short jean shorts clad ass. "I gave you the choice."

"Ah!" She flails even more, trying to get me to let go, but I still don't. "Put me down!"

"Are you going to be a good girl and follow?" I open the door to the penthouse still holding her tight. Every part of her body that touches mine sends electricity through me. I feel like my whole being is buzzing for her.

"Yes! Okay? Yes! Just put me down!"

"Okay, but if you try taking off running, hitting me, or kicking me, you're going right back up like this, and I'm biting your sexy ass instead of slapping it. Got me?"

"Fine! Put me down!"

I set her down in front of a door that leads to the roof. "Let's go." I open the door using my access, and take her hand.

She yanks it away. "I can walk on my own, thank you."

"Then walk, princess."

"Ugh! Why won't you stop calling me that?"

"Because I'm a fucking asshole." I point to the stairs.

She glances up them before she starts climbing. "What are you planning to do? Throw me off the roof?"

I grin and follow, my eyes on her ass. "The thought crossed my mind, but I'd miss your smart mouth."

She barks out a laugh. "Right."

I reach down and adjust myself because my hard on is becoming painful. Once we reach the top, I tear my eyes away from her ass and reach around her. Secured access to get in and out. This building is one of the most secure buildings in the world for a reason. Once I finish the steps to get through, I open the door for her.

"Close your eyes first," I say suddenly on a whim before I open the door all of the way.

She turns and looks at me suspiciously. "Why?"

I grin. "So you don't see when I push you off the roof."

"You're such a dick." She closes her eyes.

"I definitely have one. Pretty damn good size, too."

"Ugh!" she wrinkles her nose as I put one hand over her eyes. After I nudge her out and the door closes behind us, I rest a hand on her hip.

"Just trust me. I have something to show you, and I think you'll really like it."

"Okay."

I guide her to the edge of the pool before removing my hand. "It took a little while to make it safe, but open your eyes." I let my other hand drop to her other hip just because I really want to feel her again in any way I can.

"I… thought you said there wasn't a pool."

I smile. "When you asked about it, it was off-limits. But I called Josh that night and asked if there was anything we could do to make it safe enough for you to use. Something like with the jacuzzi."

She doesn't step away, but she does turn towards me. "Cole… This is honestly the sweetest thing. You really made this happen just so I can use it?" She looks up at me. Her pretty, hazel eyes look even more golden as they shine with unshed tears. For the first time in almost a week, she gives me a look that doesn't scream how much she hates me.

I squeeze her hips lightly and nod just a little. "You said you liked to use it for a workout, too." I keep my eyes locked on hers and catch myself leaning down a little. For some reason, I don't stop myself.

Her eyes grow a little softer and heavier, making them look sultry. "You remembered…"

"Yeah, I remembered." I lean down a little more until my lips are almost touching hers. It's like a magnet. I'm not sure I could stop myself even if I wanted to.

"Oh my God." Dylan takes a giant step back, but she's too close to the edge of the pool. She steps off the edge and loses her balance. "Ah!" she squeaks, grabbing for me.

Luckily, I'm still close enough that even though I had quickly let go of her when she stepped back, I can still easily catch her before she falls in. "I got you." I pull her against me as she grips my shirt like a lifeline. Once she's steady, I let her go and step back myself. "Uh… yeah. Anyway, the pool is available. I'm sorry to say you can't be up here yourself, but I'll leave you alone. I won't bother you."

"Oh. O-okay. Th-thank you. Um… It's a little cold for the pool today." She hugs herself and shivers.

I furrow my brows because it's not cold at all. It's even a little on the humid side, and there's a warm breeze. "Okay. Sure. We can go back downstairs."

She keeps her eyes on her feet and her distance from me. "Thank you." She briskly walks to the door, shivering for good measure.

I follow her, confused, and start to wonder if she's sick. I use my access to open the door but stay silent. She hurries down the stairs as quickly as she can with her ankle, which is getting better. I keep up without issue, but I'm trying to figure out what happened. Was it the almost kiss?

When we get into the penthouse, she beelines for the bathroom like she's trying to get away from me. I reach for her, grabbing her arm. "Hey, wait a second."

She tenses under my touch and looks up at me like she's about to cry. "What?"

I let my hand slide down her arm to her wrist. "What happened up there?"

She shakes her head. "Nothing. I'm fine. I just got cold. Maybe I'll take a hot shower. It should warm me up." She tries to pull away, but I don't let her go.

I step closer. "I'm sorry about almost kissing you. That was out of line."

Something I can't quite place flashes in her eyes. Hurt? It can't be. "Would it have been that bad?" She shakes her head again and tries to pull away once more. "Who am I kidding? That was a stupid question. Of course it would've been. It would've been a mistake, right?"

I'm not sure what about those words gets to me, but I feel like she punched me in the nuts. I drop her wrist and glare. "You're the one who pulled away from me, princess."

She steps back a few steps and holds her wrist to her chest like I hurt her as she meets my glare. "Good thing I did, huh?"

"What the fuck is that supposed to mean?"

She shrugs. "Just glad I didn't fuck something up. Make a mistake." She turns on her heel and almost runs to the bathroom.

"You can make your own dinner!" I call after her.

She doesn't answer, and I don't move until I hear the bathroom door slam. Knowing her well enough to know she'll stay in there for as long as it takes for the water to get cold, I set to cooking dinner. The intention is to just cook myself something, but I can't bring myself to actually do it. So, while the asparagus is steaming and chicken is baking, I clean up the kitchen and grab a plate for her, too.

Once it's finished, I make her plate and put it in the oven on warm. I make sure it's covered so it doesn't dry out, then eat in the kitchen standing up as I watch the sunset. It casts brilliant colors over the lake, and I can't help thinking how Dylan might like to sketch it.

Her book is sitting on the chair I forced her out of just a little while ago. All she has is a pencil, so once I finish eating, I send a text to one of our guards to get her colored drawing pencils. I'm sure there's some kind of a difference between regular ones and what she'd use, so I make sure to specify that and tell him to go to a craft shop or something to get the right kind.

I finish the rest of the dishes and then make her bed. I really want to look at the kinds of things she sketches, but not even I'm a big enough asshole to invade her privacy. If she doesn't want me to see, there has to be a reason.

I grab a bottle of water from the fridge and the notepad I use to leave her notes and for my own thoughts that I can pass on to Lance or Dane to get me the fuck out of this.

Drink the water, I write. *You need to hydrate after a shower that long and hot. Dinner's in the oven on warm. Make sure you shut the oven off.*

I leave the entire notepad next to the water bottle and head directly to my room when I hear the water shut off. I close the door quietly behind me and grab a blanket off the bed. Leaving the shades open, I lay on the couch instead of the bed. It's where I've been sleeping every night since we got here. Many times, I've tried to give her the bedroom, but every time I try, I can't get the words out because I'm trying to keep her at a distance.

Almost kissing her was a huge mistake on my part. It's a good thing she stopped it, and it's something I'll be telling myself over and over. She deserves a lot better than what I can give her.

I'm not capable of falling in love. I don't want to be hurt again. I almost didn't survive the first time. I refuse to go through that again.

Even if Dylan is everything I could ever want.

It can't happen.

It won't.

Chapter Seven

☙ Dylan ☙

I let out a sigh of relief when I see Cole isn't in the living room when I come out of the shower after time in the pool the next day. True to his word, he didn't bother me at all. He turned a pool chair around and looked out at the city the whole time I was doing laps. When I told him I was done, he didn't say a word. He got up, turned the chair around, and walked behind me the whole way back to the penthouse. When we got inside, he went to the kitchen and grabbed something to drink. Then went to his room.

Just like a bodyguard.

It's for the best. I don't know why he almost kissed me yesterday. No matter how much I want him to do it, I'm sure it would make everything worse. This past week has been absolute hell. We barely speak. When we do, we argue about something stupid. Like him calling me princess. I hate being called princess so much, but I really hate that when he does it, it makes me feel special.

I curl up in a chair and take out my new phone. A couple of days after we got here, I got a new phone delivered along with my laptop and eReader. Lance told me everything was all protected, but he was glad he took it because there were trackers on everything. I never would've known. I'm not even sure who put them there or why.

I see an email come up on my phone from my dad. "Well, that's not weird. He's never emailed me." I open the email and quickly start reading it.

My Little Girl,
I don't want you to be afraid when things start happening that don't make sense. It's entirely my fault, and I'm sorry. I got into some bad business several years ago. I thought I was doing what was best. I didn't realize I was signing you away.

"What?" I shake my head as my heart starts beating faster and dropping into my stomach at the same time. "Cole!" I yell. Something isn't right, but I keep reading.

You'll be safe with the Lucinios. They are the reason I let you go to Chicago. Being in their backyard brought you the protection I failed to give you.

Panic starts to rise. "Cole!" I yell again as I jump up and start running towards his room.

He opens the door right when I start banging on it. "Fuck, Dylan. What?" He's rubbing his eyes and isn't wearing a shirt. I'm sure he was taking a nap, but this is more important.

I push my phone at him. "My dad just emailed, and I'm freaking out!"

He squints at my phone before taking it. He starts reading the part I already read outloud, but every word that comes after chills me to my core. "You see, your mother was to marry someone else. Someone she didn't want to be with. We met at a function and hit it off. We made plans for her to come to Texas to be with me. She faked her death. I helped her stage it. I found out that very day that she was pregnant with you. She left a pregnancy test on the counter for your father to see, and we took off."

I drop to my knees and start crying. "Oh my God, Cole... What's happening?"

He kneels next to me and puts an arm around me. "There's more, but it looks like it cuts off. Want me to keep reading?"

I nod and bury my face in my hands as I take a deep breath. "I want to know." I don't know if I do or not. My chest hurts. I feel like I'm having a heart attack.

Cole starts rubbing my back. "I never wanted a kid, Dylan. But I advocated for you. She wanted to give you up. What I didn't know is that she went behind my back and did just that. She made a deal with someone, a very bad guy who agreed to buy you. You were to marry his son and form an alliance between his mafia and me, which gave him access to the Government. I got word that he was killed a few years ago. That's when I found out about the new plan. His son contacted me and said that despite his father's untimely death, the deal was still on. I'd just be directly dealing with him."

My head starts to spin as I get up. "I -"

Cole stands and helps me. His expression is completely blank, but his eyes give him away. He's scared. "My trouble was coming back to haunt me. I did some bad things before I became a Senator. Things that were hidden well. He knew. He was going to expose me if I didn't cooperate. If he did that, I'd be killed, and I wouldn't know what would happen to you or your mother." Cole pauses and looks down at me before taking a breath. "They're here. I don't have time to explain the rest. Stay with the Lucinio Mafia. Get in touch with Viper's Venom. Tell them what I said. I hope they'll figure it all out. I love you, Dylan. I wanted to break this deal. Get you away. I -" Cole takes a breath. "That's it."

I feel frozen. Like I'm standing in a giant block of ice and can't get out. I'm suffocating. I stare at him with what I'm sure are wild eyes. I don't know what to do. Cole watches me a few seconds before guiding me to his bed and sitting me down. He takes out his own phone and puts it up to his ear after he dials someone.

"Call him. I have to call him." I leap for my phone that Cole is still holding. I grab it and quickly dial his number. "Pick up. Dad, pick up. Please, please."

"Get here. Now, Josh. Bring Alec," Cole says into his phone as he watches me.

I shake my head. "Pick up. Pick up!" When it goes to his voicemail, I dial my mom. She wanted to get rid of me. It explains why she didn't seem to care about me at all. "Pick up!" I scream into the receiver.

"Jesus, Dylan. What the hell are you yelling about?" my mother asks.

"Where's dad! What did you do to my father?" I shriek into the phone. Cole drops his phone on the bed and comes to stand in front of me.

"Speaker," he mouths. I follow his order.

"Dylan. Sweetheart, do calm down. What is your problem? Are you doing drugs?"

"Where is my father?" I scream at her.

She laughs manically. "How would I possibly know that?"

"Tell me where he is!" I shriek. "Tell me!" She only keeps laughing at me. I grow more and more frantic. Cole takes my phone and hangs up. "What are you doing?" I try to grab it.

He holds it high above my head. "She's gone, Dylan. She's gone. She's with the enemy." He wraps an arm around me. I push away from him, but he holds me closer, wrapping the other arm around me. "She's gone," he whispers. "She's the enemy now."

"No! No, that's not possible! She's lying! She knows where he is!"

Cole hugs me tighter. "I know. I know. But she's not going to tell us. She's with Ethan. She's with the enemy."

"Who?"

"It's a long story. He's the leader of this biker gang named Ruthless Warriors. I knew as soon as he mentioned Lucinio Mafia and Viper's Venom. His father, Matthew Lucinio, was killed by us a few years ago."

I look up at him. "Wait… Lucinio…?"

He nods slowly. "Yeah. Lucinio. Ethan is Matthew's son. Which makes him -"

"Josh's and Alex's brother."

"Half-brother. Matthew led quite the double life. Well, triple. Lance and Robby have done a lot of digging. It looks like he's the end of Matthew's line. There's honestly a lot of shit that we're all still trying to process."

I pull away from him and shake my head. "No. No, it's not possible." I turn and hurry out of his room. "It's not possible. She wouldn't do that. We have to find my dad. I have to call my cousin. Xavier will know what to do."

I hear him let out a breath and feel him following. I'm getting far too in tune to where he is. I don't know if that's a good thing or a bad thing. "I think maybe Colton would be a better option, Dylan. He's the cop, remember?"

I ignore him and call Xavier. He's always been the one I go to for everything. I love Colton, but Xavier is my person. He's the one who's always fixed everything.

"Hey, cos. What's up? Enjoying -"

"I need you to check on my dad. He just sent me an email. I'll text it to you. Something is wrong. My mom isn't answering me when I ask where he is."

"Wait. What? Slow down. What email?"

I watch Cole sit down and rub his head. "I'll send it now." I quickly pull it up and copy and paste it. I text it to him. "There. I copy and pasted and texted it. He cuts off. He says crazy stuff. Cole said something about Ethan having my mom. I -"

"Dylan? It's Colt. Is Cole there?"

"Oh, um. Yeah." I put my phone on speaker as I glance at Cole. "He's here. You're on speaker."

"Cole? Listen, man. A call came in about Foster Remington. We have officer's going out now. I'm on my way because patrol called me. I think you need to call Josh. The person who called it in was -"

"Let me guess. Ethan Lucinio," Cole says, not opening his eyes as he rubs his temples.

"How did you know that?" Colt asks.

"Because everything in that email I assume Xavier is showing you adds up to only one conclusion. A guy he was working with was killed. His son called and said he'll be dealing with him now. Deal isn't off. Her father cuts off mid-sentence like he's sending the email as someone is bursting in. I'd check his office. Second thing is her mother. Dylan asked her where her dad is. She didn't answer. Just laughed, but what was very clear was the sound of a motorcycle in the background and someone whispering to get on."

I furrow my brows. "I didn't hear that."

Cole looks at me. "Because you were screaming, princess. You were in shock."

I glare at him for the princess comment, but he gives it right back. I hate it more that I'm not even mad he calls me that. "It doesn't matter. Just please tell me what happened to my dad."

There's a long pause before Xavier finally starts speaking. "Dylan, I don't think he made it. Uh, Colt... said... the call was for a homicide."

Tears sting my eyes. My lip trembles. My hand shakes, and I drop my phone. I cover my mouth as a sob escapes. Cole bends over and picks up the phone. "Let us know," Cole says. "I have Josh and Alec coming. We need to go."

"Just... take care of her," Xavier says. "This has to be a shock to her."

I choke down another sob, but it doesn't work. Cole assures Xavier I'm safe and hangs up just as I get up. I crawl into the bed because it's the only area I feel safe. Like it's my place. My domain. Something I have control over. Something I can say to stay out of or enter. It's a small fraction of comfort, but it's something I'm going to hold onto with all my might because it's all I have right now.

I hug a pillow and cry into it. I don't even know why. Maybe it's for the total loss of any semblance of understanding of what's going on. Maybe because I can't grasp any of this. Maybe it's because I know in my heart my father is gone and my mother is responsible. Or maybe it's because my entire life and all I believed it was is no longer. Who am I? Where did I come from? If my dad wasn't really my dad, who is?

So many questions are running through my mind that I can't even grasp onto any of them. I can't think through anything. Nothing makes sense. Bits and pieces of things I've heard over the course of my life are floating in the chaos, but it's like a tornado that's so angry and large that all anyone can do is get out of the way and hope it doesn't suck them into it. There's no chance of survival with all of the spinning and jagged edges of the debris it's eaten.

When Josh and Alec show up, I pull the blankets over my head. I feel nothing. I'm numb. I'm so lost in my own thoughts, that I don't really even hear them as they talk.

I'm really what everyone says I am. Just some girl who lived a privileged life. A princess in her castle who has no idea what really goes on in the real world.

A nobody…

Chapter Eight

☞ Cole ☜

Dylan hasn't stopped crying the entire time I've been talking to Josh and Alec. I can still see her body trembling. I lean back in a chair and run a hand down my face. My normal scruff is far less trimmed because I haven't slept well since this entire bullshit all started.

"We need proof," I mumble. "I'm not going to Ink and saying anything until we know for sure. She doesn't need that. Neither does he. He struggles enough."

"I know," Alec says. "We can do DNA. I'll get his."

Josh leans forward and glances at me. "We need to get you guys home. She needs to be around Dallas and Rosie. She can't go back to Texas, but she has no family here. Just them."

"Then, get us out of here. I refuse to go back there and put my family in danger with a mob camped out front wanting my head. That needs to be dealt with. I need to be cleared. And then I can do my job and protect her while tracking down the man behind this."

"I have a couple people I'm putting on her permanently. Landon is one of them. She's comfortable with him. They've been talking."

I swallow the lump of jealousy and ignore the tightness in my chest. I do nothing more than nod and look at my watch. "It's getting late," I say. "She needs a fucking break. Just one."

Josh stands. Alec follows. "I'll get Dr. Freeman over here," Josh says. "He needs to look at her foot anyway. Make sure she's healing right."

"Just… give her tonight, man." My heart breaks a little more every time I look at her.

She's devastated.

Broken.

Josh gives me a half smile and pats my shoulder as he and Alec leave. I sit for a few minutes watching Dylan. She's been underneath the covers the entire time we've been talking. Every now and then, her hand darts out to grab the phone she's put on her pillow, then slips back out to put it back. I have no doubt she's talking to Landon, Rosie, and Dallas. Probably her cousins, too. Maybe she has a group chat. Maybe individual. I don't know.

I sigh as I stand slowly. I walk to the fridge to find her something to drink. I settle on a bottle of red gatorade and bring it back to her. I sit on the edge of the bed and reach over to the lump that is her torso. Hesitating momentarily, I lay my hand on her hip, still holding the Gatorade in the other hand.

"Who's Ink?" she asks quietly.

Straight for the balls. I see how this is going to go. I let out a whoosh of a breath. "Maybe we should start from the beginning."

"I already know about Matthew Lucinio. Dallas told me. Who's Ink?"

I let out another breath and swallow. "He's a Captain with Viper's Venom."

"What does that mean? He's the leader or something?"

I chuckle and squeeze her hip a little, just to show comfort. "No. He's third in command. Not just of the Chicago chapter. He's third in command of the entire Viper's Venom organization nationally."

"What does he have to do with me?" she nearly whispers.

"That… is a story that I think you might need a little comfort and support for."

She throws the covers off with a huff. Her hair is a disaster. Her eyes are red from her tears, but she's still breathtaking. She sits up and crosses her legs in front of her. "I love my cousins, and I love Dallas and Rosie. Landon is very supportive, but I... just... I guess I need a little bit of a break." She looks down at her feet and plays with her fingernails.

I close my eyes and nod before opening them and repositioning myself so I'm facing her. "Okay. You want it all straight?"

She nods but doesn't meet my eyes. I'm not touching her anymore, and I'm kicking myself for missing the feel of her. "Straight," she whispers.

"Several years ago, before I even knew who he was, hell, before I was even involved in any of this in any capacity, Ink came home one day to his entire family gone. He was young. He had a young girlfriend. He was probably around twenty or something, but he made good money. He didn't exactly do it the legal way, but he had money, and it wasn't long after that when Alec took over Viper's Venom and made it all legal. It was a few years later. At that time, though, it was run by Alec's father. Ink had his own place, mostly because of Alec. He was ready to start a life with his high school sweetheart. It seemed to be what she wanted, too. He proposed. Everything was fine. He came home from a mission with Alec, though, and she was gone. Vanished. With the amount of blood he found, though, it fucked him up. He thought she'd been killed."

"That's... really sad."

"It gets worse for him. After he saw all of that, he also saw a pregnancy test placed on the counter. He always thought it was a sign from her. He believed she wasn't dead, but that she'd been taken. He thought Alec's father sold her. He had no idea what truly happened, but there were a lot of theories. Their relationship was good. They never fought. She seemed happy, so there was no reason to believe she'd taken off. Over the years, though, he started to lose hope, until one day he had to come to the realization that he'd never know the truth. It fucked him up. And then you had that conversation with Dallas and Rosie that brought Josh and Alec down to Texas."

She nods slowly. "Yeah..." She twists her fingers and rubs them.

Unable to resist and knowing she needs it, I reach over and take both of her hands in mine. "Do you want me to keep going?"

"I want to know..." She studies my hand as I hold hers. My hand is so much bigger than hers. I can fit both of hers in mine.

"When you called Dallas and Rosie about the conversation you overheard, it put us all on alert. And nothing at all made sense after that. Your father went from that conversation to being the doting and supportive father. No one thought that was normal behavior. Especially when Dallas told us he hated the very idea of you going anywhere other than Texas to college. My theory is that he had a falling out with Ethan and wanted to back out on the deal, but he got threatened. He knows we're up here, so he started supporting you in wanting to come up here to go to Chicago. You'd have protection. Your best friend was adopted by two very powerful men. You would have the police, all of Josh's allies, and that includes Viper's Venom." I take a breath. "His email... uh... well, it clinched it for me. I don't know the mystery behind it, but your dad gave me enough to not let it go. With it in Josh's hands now, it can be investigated in ways I can't do, especially right now since I'm on leave."

"You... think... he's my real dad..."

I nod and give her hand a gentle squeeze. "Things add up. My job is to put pieces together. The pieces fit. Now, I need to prove or disprove it. But it makes sense. Your dad was talking about your mom getting away from a dirty biker and being pregnant. He was talking about her finding out she was pregnant that day. Personally, I think she did know and went along with the plan because she didn't want you. I'm not exactly sure what the play was on her end, but if she didn't want you, then going along with his plan makes sense."

She sniffles. I feel like she has a grip on my heart and is squeezing it. "I honestly feel like I just have no place in the world right now. That everything everyone says about me is true. I'm just a nobody who lived a privileged life. I've heard that over and over and over again. Xavier and my cousins were always my protectors. When they were around, no one messed with me, but I was a year behind them. I was two years behind Xavier. When they were gone and I was a Senior, things changed. It didn't matter that I was the head cheerleader. It didn't matter that I was part of a team that went to championships and won them. It didn't matter I was a straight A student. It didn't matter I was accepted to a top ten university. Nothing mattered anymore. Just that I was Foster Remington's daughter." She sniffles and grips my hand a little tighter. "And now I don't even have that. My cousins aren't really my cousins. My uncles aren't my uncles. My grandparents aren't mine. I have nothing. No one. I don't know where I came from or who I am. Why didn't Ink look for me?"

"I don't know, sweetheart. I don't have all of those answers. I know that Cain, Ink's real name, did look for your mom for a while, but he really thought she was dead when no trace of her ever came up. We found out that her name was changed. They'll have Lance look into it more, but it looks like there was no trace of her because everything about her and her old identity was erased. She was given a whole new identity. I'm sure Matthew had a hand in that. I don't know why he didn't take you when you were born, but there has to be some reason for it. Some kind of deal he made. We just need to figure it out. As for you, I can't even begin to imagine how hard this is for you."

"Everything is just gone. Ripped away. I never felt a lot of love from my mom, but I did from my dad. He was strict, but I never doubted he loved me. Even with the weird conversations I've heard, I still never doubted his love for me. I guess I don't know how to think right now. I don't know much of anything right now."

Her hair falls in front of her face. I reach over and push it back. "I don't blame you for that."

She looks up at me, her eyes puffy. "You're being nice."

I grin. "I have my moments. I'm not a dick all of the time."

She gives me a weak smile before looking down again. "I like this you."

I'm sure she doesn't mean for her words to kick me in my heart, but they do just that. "How about I make us dinner, and we just hang out and watch a movie or something? You pick."

She smiles and looks at me shyly. "I can pick anything?"

I groan and roll my eyes. "What the hell did I just get into?"

She giggles. "*My Little Pony*?"

I laugh. "Okay, no. Not anything. Not that. Overruled. Vetoed."

"What about *Barbie*?" Her eyes light up.

"The new one? With Margot Robbie I think her name is?"

"Yes. That one."

"Sure." I let her hands go as I stand. "As long as *Oppenheimer* is next."

"Ooh! Yes. I've wanted to see that one for a while. Can we have tacos and all things junk food?"

I laugh. "Sure. Anything to make you smile."

I get out everything I need to make tacos as she looks for the movies. As I'm preparing it all, she makes her bed. I'm doing all I can to keep my focus on the food instead of her. She's so fucking beautiful. Everything about her appeals to me. It's gone far beyond physical. I love her personality. I love how just one smile can change everything for me. It can make my day. A glare from her makes me hate that I fucked up, but the asshole part of me never lets me apologize, even though I know I should.

I turn away from her when she grabs the Gatorade and starts walking towards me. She opens the fridge and puts it away but pulls out another one. "I assume you wanted me to drink this to hydrate after all of the crying?" she asks softly.

"Uh…" I clear my throat and make a conscious effort to control what I swear is becoming teenage hormones. "Yeah, but I forgot to give it to you. I was too busy trying to do the comfort thing."

"Thank you for that." She looks down at the bottle she's fiddling with in her hands. "Do you want something?"

"There's a bottle of sweet tea in there. I'll take that."

She smiles at me, and I fucking melt. It's impossible not to smile back, but I do have enough control to not let her see I'm checking out her ass when she bends over to get the bottle out of the fridge. She closes it and takes them both to the living room.

"Can we kind of make this like a…" She trails off.

I look at her while I start putting the tacos together. "Can we make this a what?"

"Never mind. It was stupid."

I narrow my eyes as she puts the drinks on the coffee table. "I'm sure it wasn't stupid. Also, don't let me hear that out of your mouth again." When I finish putting the tacos together I bring them to the table on a serving platter and go back for plates. "What were you going to say? Whatever it was, you seemed excited about it."

"It's nothing. Really."

I come back with plates and sit on a chair opposite her as she starts pulling up the movie. "You know I'm not dropping this."

She keeps her full attention on her plate and the tacos as she takes a couple and puts them on her plate. After a few moments, she smiles at me. "It's really okay. Thank you for making tacos."

"You're welcome. I'm still not dropping it. Talk to me."

She signs and plays with her plate. "You're going to think it's stupid and make fun of me for even saying such a thing. And you'd be right."

"I promise I won't think it's stupid, and I swear, Dylan, if you keep talking like that, I'm not going to hold back with the spanking." I level her with a dominant stare.

Her eyes widen. She clears her throat and presses her thighs together, though I'm positive it was all an unconscious effort. "Fine," she whispers, looking down once more. "I... thought... maybe we could... sit together." She nods to the bed. "Just... be friends. At least friendly. For a little while, anyway."

"Okay."

Her eyes snap to mine, shock registering in them and making them glitter. "Really?" she asks hesitantly.

I bite my lip and give her a half smile. "Really." I take my tacos as she gets up. She balances her plate as she crawls into the bed. I set my plate down and take the empty tray of tacos back to the kitchen where I grab a lap table we can use to put our stuff on. I bring it with me to the bed and set it down at the edge. "Can you hold my plate for a minute?"

"Mmhmm." She takes it when I hand it to her. I quickly grab a second comforter and our drinks.

I set the drinks on the bed as I crawl into it, then arrange the blanket over us both. I've learned she really likes wrapping herself in blankets. I thought it was just because she wanted to annoy me with the temp in the penthouse, but that wasn't it. They make her feel content and safe. She's in her happy place when she's burrowed into a blanket with a book.

When I finish with the blanket, she's smiling, happier than I've seen her in days. It makes my heart beat a little faster. I set the lap table up for us. I don't mind at all that we have to sit pretty close to fit it over both of our laps comfortably. She sets my plate and hers on the table as I set our drinks down.

"Is this what you wanted?" I half-tease, half really want to know if I'm doing it right.

"It's perfect. Thank you. I just... don't really want to be alone right now."

I look down at her feeling honest to hell stabs of pain. "If I could take any of this away, I'd do it, princess," I say before I can stop myself.

She smiles a little as she nods. She doesn't say anything else as she turns the movie on. I watch her for a few more moments before I turn and focus on the start of the movie. We both eat in silence, but throughout the movie, she's smiling more and more. She tears up when some of the songs come on, but when the movie nears its end, she seems to be feeling a lot better.

I can't even come close to imagining what she's going through. I don't know what I'd be like if I lost all I knew. My whole identity.

Maybe it's time for me to turn over a new leaf and open myself up to at least getting to know her a little bit. Talk to her instead of just observing her for her likes and dislikes; her passions and loves.

I suck in a breath at where my thoughts just went. For the first time in a very, very long time, I'm content with a woman. It's something I haven't felt with anyone since... I subtly shake the thoughts away. I won't think of *her*. She's always lingering in the back of my head somewhere making me fear taking things anywhere with women who aren't her.

Dylan is so different. She looks nothing like her. She doesn't act like her. Dylan is genuine, and no matter how hard I've been on her, it wasn't me who ended up breaking her.

Maybe, just maybe, she'll let me be the one to help put her back together.

Piece by beautiful piece...

Chapter Nine

☙ Dylan ❧

"So, wait. Wasn't Oppenheimer also responsible for something to do with food in Germany and poisoning?"

Cole grins. "Kind of. He responded to a proposal regarding it. He said they couldn't move forward with the project unless they were certain they could poison half a million men."

"But why would he do that? I mean who's to say that doesn't get to women and children?"

"The idea was that it would be going directly to the military, but you're right. There was no guarantee."

I shiver in disgust. "We only really learned a fraction of this in school. I wish we could've learned more and all been as absolutely grossed out as I am now."

I lean into him, and he puts his arm comfortably around my shoulders. "If they'd taught all of this in school, you would've had a class completely dedicated to just this war. Not just US History or World History."

"This is all just a blip. That's the sad thing. The school system is just broken."

He rubs his hand soothingly on my arm as I grab another nacho. We decided to go all out with snacks. We have nachos, Oreos, and popcorn. Cole even grabbed sodas for us.

"It's really a shame to hear that. When I was in school, we learned a lot of stuff that doesn't seem to be taught anymore."

"Some of us did our own research on a lot of stuff, like slavery, but they really don't teach things that should be. I know a girl who graduated with me who can't name the fifty states and has no idea what continents are or what they're called. She doesn't know the difference between a state and country. It's really sad. I think they just expect parents to teach that stuff, but then what's the purpose of school?"

"Legitimate question." He hugs me closer, and I melt as the movie continues.

After a few moments, I sigh. "I feel like we should've watched Barbie after this."

"In hindsight, yes. I agree." He looks down at me. "Want to shut it off and watch something else?"

I look up at him. "Would you mind? I could go for a good thriller."
He grins. "Are you a thriller lover?"
I smile brightly and nod. "I love thrillers."
"What's your favorite?"

"My favorite right now is *The Coven*, but I really like *Shutter Island, Buried, The Beekeeper*. Oh! *Nowhere* and *Somewhere Quiet* are super good."

"*Shutter Island* is one of my favorites." He stops *Oppenheimer* and searches for *Shutter Island*. "These nachos are fucking fantastic. Where did you learn to do them like this?"

I smile up at him. "We visited Montana once when we were younger. All of us cousins with our parents. They had this place called Taco Johns. We figured it was like Taco Bell, but it's so much better. They made them with refried beans, meat or chicken, and then had these amazing toppings. I wonder if there's one in Chicago. It's a midwestern thing, I think. They aren't a national chain."

"Well, they're really good. I'll definitely have to look and see if they're here later on. Not now. I really just want to relax and not think of anything outside this room."

"So, this isn't the time to be bringing up how I still feel like a nobody?" I ask softly looking down at the blankets.

I feel him rest his chin on my head as he turns on the movie. "You know you're anything but. I know this has to be hard for you, but it doesn't really change you as a person. You're still smart. You're still beautiful and creative. You're still a cheerleader. And you might not think it... your cousins might not be related to you by blood, but I don't think they're going to shun you. You still have them. Foster Remington might not have been the best guy, but he still raised you. You said it yourself that you felt love from him. I think that letter showed that he knows how much he fucked up, but he loves you enough to have tried to get you out of it by getting you here where he knew you had a chance."

I absently draw patterns on his muscular thigh as I think. I don't say anything until we're almost halfway through the movie, and when I do, I still focus on the blankets and his thigh. "Do you really think all of that?" I almost whisper.

He runs his fingers through my hair. "Yes. No matter what the secrets behind the curtain are, you still lived the life you led. You still achieved all that you did. None of that changes."

"Maybe... but my family -"

"Is still your family. I'll be honest, princess. If they drop out of your life, they aren't worthy of you. They don't know what they're missing. They don't deserve the honor of having you in their life, let alone breathing the air you do. It's times like this where you really find out who your true friends are. Who's really there for you. Only the strongest survive stuff like this. I don't doubt you have it in you to become an even tougher person than you are already. Whether anyone is going to be standing by your side when the dust settles is something we're going to have to find out. The people who are will be the people you can always trust."

"You're really smart," I say after a few moments of letting his words soak in as I continue my patterns on his thigh. I don't know why it soothes me, but it does. I've never done it before, but I've never had anyone who let me cuddle with them either.

Cole chuckles and takes my hand in his while simultaneously pulling me closer with the other. "Smart enough to know that if you trace patterns any higher, you're going to end up with a surprise I'm pretty sure you don't want."

For the first time in a good hour, I notice Cole is quite hard, and a lot bigger than I thought. Apparently, gray sweatpants aren't the only thing he shows prominently in. "Oh." I look away quickly and attempt to sit up.

"I didn't say you had to get up, now." Cole's voice is lower. Whenever it drops like that, it does things between my thighs that only I've ever done. And it's not the same. It's far more intense.

"I'm s-sorry. I wasn't paying attention. I'll keep my hands to myself." I look up at him shyly with a tinge of embarrassment coloring my cheeks.

He smirks. "I didn't say don't touch either. I just said I'm pretty sure you don't want it, but judging from how you keep casting your eyes down and looking at it, and how your hand is trembling in mine, maybe I'm wrong. I've been wrong before. Rarely, but it's happened."

This time, I do let my eyes drop. I'd rather look at his dick and his thumb rubbing circles over the back of my hand than in his eyes that are burning their way into my soul. "What if I do want it?"

"Then, I'm not gonna stop you." He gives my hand a squeeze before he puts it on his thigh and goes back to rubbing my arm soothingly. Only this time, he also plays with my hair. It's another thing I didn't realize how much I love until this moment.

A few minutes more of watching the movie, and I take a chance I can't believe I'm taking. Instead of tracing his thigh, I trace the outline of his cock. Part of me expects him to shove me away. I know there's no way I'm the type of girl he's used to. I'm not anyone's type of girl. I'm too short. I'm not as toned as I should be. My boobs aren't as perky. They probably aren't even the right size. My butt's too big. I'm not perfect like all of the blond, blue-eyed cheerleaders who make it to the big leagues, like the Dallas Cowboys. I'm sure that's why things didn't work out with the guy I lost my virginity to. I wasn't good enough.

But Cole's soft breaths and low moans spur me on anyway. "Fuck...," he rumbles as his head falls back.

I bite my lip, fascinated at him. I open my hand and press my palm to his length. I rub my thumb across his tip slowly and revel in another moan from deep within him. His fingers tangle in my hair. I look up at him as I bring my hand up to his waistband. I pause at the button and wait. I'm not sure if it's permission I seek, or if I'm silently begging him for some kind of leadership. Maybe it's both. I've never done this before. My sexual experience is very limited to two minutes of uncomfortable intercourse that I got nothing from but some soreness.

Without taking his eyes off mine or his fingers out of my hair, Cole unbuttons his jeans. He holds himself down as I slowly unzip them. He's mesmerizing. No matter how hard I try to look away, I drown deeper and deeper in his eyes until I have no hope of surfacing for air.

I watch him get closer and closer, but I'm convinced I'm imagining it. That is until his lips, manly and rough, meet my soft ones. His stubble brushes against my skin. Everywhere he touches makes it feel like tiny explosions are happening. Electricity seems to zip through me. My eyes fall closed on their own, and I melt into the kiss.

I grip the waistband of his jeans with one hand and gasp when I feel him press his dick into my other hand. It's enough for him to slip his tongue into my mouth and moan. He takes my hand in his and closes it around his cock. He feels like the hardest of metals wrapped in the softest of silks. His hand, calloused and definitely used, stays closed around mine and starts stroking his dick up and down with it, guiding me. Slowly but hard. His hips arch into me, and I take that as his way of saying he likes it.

"Just like that, baby," he whispers as he kisses down my jaw to my neck. "Keep going just like that." His deep voice reverberates against my neck, sending shivers through my entire body.

"Okay," I whisper.

He shifts and turns his body more towards me. It's enough to let me slip my other arm around him while still stroking his length. I press my lips against his neck. He keeps one arm wrapped around me. The other is moving up and down my leg and slipping under the leg of my jean shorts. Sometimes, he squeezes my ass. Other times, he allows his thumb to brush over my already damp panties.

I start rotating my wrist as I stroke him, and I arch into him. I want more. I need it. I just don't know what. Me on his lap? Should I try that? Should I stroke him with both hands? He's so big, long, and hard.

Just when I make the decision to move, Cole drives one long finger into my aching pussy at the same time his lips meet mine again. He swallows my moan of pleasure. I spread my legs for him as he works around my shorts and panties. When my head falls back, he follows, still dominating me and the kiss.

"Cole…," I whisper as his finger pumps inside of me and out. He moves it in a circle and crookes in against a spot that makes me burst into tingles, but when he puts his thumb against my clit and presses as he rubs, my thighs tremble. "Cole!" My pussy clenches around his finger. It pulses and gets wetter and wetter for him.

Following his lead, I start stroking him faster. "Good girl," he rumbles as his dick thickens impossibly more in my hand. "Keep going, princess." He tugs my hair and presses his lips to mine once more, stealing my breath; my heart, melting me with the heat of it.

The possessiveness and pure alpha dominance makes something inside me snap. I scream into his mouth as my body tenses. My pussy spasms as my body goes through convulsions. I grip his shirt so tight, I'm completely shocked I don't rip it. I ride his thrusts like I would a horse that's galloping towards a cliff. I hold on with everything I am as he careens me off the ground and into the unknown.

When I finally safely touch the ground again, Cole pulls away from the kiss slowly. Suddenly, I feel his dick in my hand again. I don't know if I stopped stroking him, but I'm currently still doing it rapidly. He's thrusting into my hand with rumbles of satisfaction. He's warm in my hand. The tip of his cock is red and leaking something I'm sure is precome.

Cole watches me as he pulls his finger out of my pussy. He puts it in his mouth, and I realize all at once that it's me he's sucking off himself.

The urgency to taste him has me quickly repositioning myself so I can take him in my mouth. I close my eyes the second I have my mouth around him and moan as I suck the precome beading at his tip.

"Jesus fuck, sweet girl." Cole's body trembles just enough for me to know I'm doing something right. His stomach tightens. His fingers tangle in my hair once more. "Baby, I'm gonna come." He tries to tug me back, but I shake my head. I want to taste him. If he tastes anything like his precome, he'll become my new addiction.

"Mmm…," I moan again, this time in complete contentment as I flick his tip with my tongue while I suck.

"Oh, fuck yes." Jets of his essence start shooting into my mouth. I swallow and take him deeper until his dick is touching the back of my throat. I swallow around him, causing him to jerk his hips into me. "Holy Christ, baby."

Once I've greedily taken all he gives me, I pull off him just as slowly as he pulled his finger out of me. I move to my knees and fold my hands in my lap. For some reason completely unknown to me, I need him to tell me I did a good job. That it felt good for him and was enjoyable.

I lick my lip and wait. He groans as he watches me and pulls me to him. His kiss is hot, dominating, and exudes possessiveness. The possessiveness I crave. The need to feel like I'm his and no one else's. He presses me against the back of the couch and deepens the kiss. The taste of me on his tongue intermingles with his own taste on mine. I can't get enough. I press even closer to him, taking everything he'll allow me to have.

Several moments, or maybe years, later, Cole pulls away slowly. His eyes. I love his eyes. I love how whenever he looks at me, they're like my own, personal inferno. Something he reserves just for me.

But I still need to know if I made him happy. If I did all I could to please him. So, I clear my throat and let my fingers settle on his perfect abs. "Did… I… do good?" I whisper, ashamed at how lame that actually sounded out loud.

"So fucking good," he whispers back with a sexy smile. "So fucking good, princess."

I smile and close my eyes again when his lips touch mine in a kiss that's as sweet as it is panty melting. "Will you stay here with me?" I ask, unable to meet the eyes that I've somehow fallen in love with.

"You could ask me to be the cause of the third world war, and I'd do it. I'd do anything you asked me to."

I don't need to see the blush to know it's somehow covering my entire body. I feel flushed enough to want to hide in him. I don't know if the movie is even playing still, but it doesn't matter because all I want is for him to hug me like he is.

Protective.

Like no one can touch me but him.

Like in order to get to me, they have to go through him.

I don't believe anyone, Ruthless Warriors or an entire Army, could get through him. He makes me feel like he's impenetrable. I'll never be alone or vulnerable with him by my side.

Chapter Ten

☙ Cole ☙

(One Week Later)

It's only been a week of what I consider pure bliss. Dylan has gotten to talk to her cousins. They've all reassured her that they aren't abandoning her. She's still struggling with the loss of her father, but it has been proven that Cain, or Ink, as he's known in the VV, really is her father. She wants to meet him, but we need to stay where we are and keep lying low. No one knows where Ethan is, but I believe he's here in Chicago. No one has spotted him, though, and we have many, many eyes looking for him.

Beyond all of that, Dylan and I are getting along very well. I haven't let down my defenses, but we're at least on speaking terms, and I've woken up next to her every single morning since our movie night, which we've had more of. I love getting to know her. She's as vivacious and driven as she is sexy and smart. I've never been challenged by anyone on an intellectual level like I am with her.

That's not the only reason things are going so well, though. I might have met my match on all levels, including sexually. She's not afraid to tell me when she needs something. If she's not getting the attention she wants, she simply takes it. It's not a bad thing. I tend to get immersed in my work and my own head, so I appreciate that she recognizes it and pulls me out of it all.

"Do you think I'll make tryouts?" she asks quietly from a chair she's reading in. She doesn't look at me. I'm sure she thinks the answer is going to be no.

"I don't honestly know, baby. I -" The ring of my ringtone cuts me off at the same time hers does. I furrow my brows and pick up my phone as she picks up hers. I already have a bad feeling.

"I don't know this number," she whispers as she looks at me.

I look down at my phone. "I don't either." I signal her to answer it as I do the same. "Hello?" we both say in unison.

"I'm coming for you. I hope you don't think being locked up in that tower is going to stop me. That compound of yours isn't impenetrable."

Dylan looks at her phone and me in horror. I hold up a hand to keep her silent. "What the hell is your play, Ethan?"

He laughs. "Isn't it obvious? I want to finish what my father started. Only his plan was to overpower you all. Mine is much better. Take out the ranked members and watch you all fall down. Weaken the chain of command, and everyone is crippled."

I grin a little wickedly. "You think if you go after me and systematically destroy Josh by taking out the higher ups is really going to stop us? Come on, now. You have to be smarter than that and know we have safeguards."

"You mean the Crane Mafia? And how they'd just absorb yours and become larger? Nah. I don't buy that. There's no one to take over for Josh. And once I take you out, I'm going for your partner. Then, I'll take out the most important people in Josh's life, starting with his little bitch girlfriend. She looks like my type. But before I do any of that, you're going to hand over the pretty little old lady you have with you because she belongs to me."

Those words make my protective instincts and dark side snap into place like a second skin. I glare as Dylan curls into a ball crying silent tears. "Let's get one thing straight, motherfucker. You're not going anywhere near her. There's a reason I hold the position I do in this organization. It's not because I'm a cop."

"Yeah, but that badge certainly has you all tied up, pretty boy."

"Good thing I don't hide behind my shield, huh? Where are you?"

"You think I'm gonna tell you that, tracker boy? Not a chance. I will say this, though. That sexy little minx sitting on that couch right now looking all terrified would look pretty sexy sucking my cock like she loves to do with yours."

My eyes are instantly on the window. Dylan freezes. I get up and move to shield her. "You're gonna have to go through me to get anywhere near her." My eyes scan the buildings surrounding us, but I see no signs anywhere of anyone watching us. Dylan's hand grips the waistband of my jeans as she hides behind me.

"You think that's gonna be hard?" Ethan hangs up. I keep systematically scanning buildings.

"Oh my God, Cole. What do we do?"

"Call Josh. Do it now."

"Yes, sir."

Standing like this in front of the window leaves me wide open for attack, but these windows are bulletproof. It would take one hell of a powerful weapon to get through. We're more protected in this building than we are in the Headquarters building. The glass on the windows is thicker.

Just then, I catch movement in an upper floor of a hotel a few buildings down from where we are. I don't lead on that I see anything, but I do reach for a remote. With one button, the shades are closing. I could put us in lockdown, but I'm taking a gamble that Ethan isn't as fucking smart as I am.

"Josh? It's me. Dylan. We have a problem. Ethan. He's near. He knows where we are."

As soon as the shades are drawn, I move to the window. I have a pair of binoculars sitting on an end table next to the window. I grab them and move the shade just a sliver so I can look closer at what I saw in the hotel.

"Yes, sir. I understand. I'll tell him." Dylan hangs up her phone and starts moving at lightning speed. "We have to pack up. He said stay in here until he gets here."

"Pack up your stuff, baby. Stay away from the windows."

"Okay." She hurries around and starts throwing all of her stuff in her bags. "What about you?"

"Don't worry about me. Do what you're told."

As suspected, there's a man in RW cuts standing at the window looking right at the penthouse. He's using binoculars just as I am, but I know he doesn't see me because he's scanning what is the gym of this penthouse looking for any signs of us. I grab the remote and close the shades in the gym, bathroom, and my bedroom simultaneously to confuse him.

Just as I wanted him, too, he puts his binoculars down and watches the shades closing. He's confused because he knows there are only two people in the penthouse. There's no way for all shades to close everywhere at exactly the same time.

"Stop," I say to Dylan when she starts reaching for something near the curtain. She freezes and turns her head towards me. "Do not, under any circumstances, touch the shades. Don't turn on any lights. Nothing."

Carefully, with shaky hands, she reaches for her laptop charger and phone charger that's plugged into the wall. Like a good girl, though, she doesn't disturb the curtains in the slightest.

I watch Ethan scanning with his binoculars and move just enough so he can't see me when he starts getting close to where I am. I close the shade without disturbing the rest of it. Dylan is watching me like a hawk for any kind of direction.

"I want you to go into my bedroom and pack my stuff. Everything is in the closet. There's nothing in the drawers. There's a few things in the bathroom. My charger is next to the nightstand. Be careful of the curtains. No lights."

She nods and scurries towards the bedroom. I very cautiously peek out the side of the shade again and scan quickly for anyone watching me from anywhere else before my eyes land back on where Ethan is. I take out my phone and put it on speaker.

"Captain Rens."

"DJ, it's me. I need anyone and everyone available to storm Hotel Grand. Top floor. Penthouse suite. There are two suites on the top level. Ethan is the one opposite the side closest to Josh's penthouse that me and Dylan are in."

"Jesus, Westwood. You can't be serious."

"Dead serious. I'm looking right at him." I put the binoculars up to my eyes again. Ethan has his back turned to me. I can see he's talking to another guy, but next to him is a female with dark hair and a drool worthy body. She's wearing next to nothing. Just short shorts and a crop top.

"Okay. Stay away from this. I just got put in position last week. I don't need anything fucked up by a Sergeant on admin leave."

"I'm not going in, Cap. I can see Ethan talking to someone. I know there are two other guys and a female in there, but I don't know if anyone else is there."

"Confirmed four males, one female, correct?"

"Yes. One of the males is Ethan for sure."

"I'll expedite a warrant and send teams."

"Be quick. We're leaving from the other side, but they'll catch on that we aren't here."

"I'll have it within the hour. Already putting it in. We'll be storming it by the time you're leaving. Who's the girl?"

"Unsure. Give me a minute." I turn to call for Dylan, but it's like she knows she's needed. She appears carrying my bags. "Come here." I go back to watching Ethan as she hurries to my side. I move back so she can stand in front of me. "I need you to look through these binoculars to the top floor of the hotel across the street. Be quick. Don't knock the shade, but tell me who the woman is. I have a feeling I know. I need confirmation."

She nods and does what I say. Seconds later, she's stepping away from me and handing me the binoculars. I quickly go back to watching. "It's my mom," she whispers.

"I thought so. She looks a lot like you."

"People thought we were sisters. She loved that."

"What's her name?" DJ asks.

"Mackenzie Remington." Dylan glances at my phone before looking back at me.

"Be quick, Cap. Looks like they're mobilizing." I watch as they start rushing around the room.

"On it." DJ hangs up.

Ethan grabs his binoculars and looks around the penthouse once more. Just like before, I close the curtain just before he gets to me. "Where's the notepad?" I ask Dylan.

"Um…" She looks around quickly. "Oh. On the kitchen counter." She rushes to it.

"Write 'fuck you' on it. See if there's any tape in one of those drawers in the kitchen."

"Okay."

While she's doing that, I glance once more out of the window and quickly scan to make sure he's not watching. I can see him enough to know he's standing in front of the window, but he doesn't have the binoculars. I put mine back up to my eyes. He's not looking in my direction. Instead, he's looking down at the road. I don't know if he thinks that's how we'll be leaving, but it's not. There are two main entrances to this building, but the entrance with a direct elevator to this floor is on the other side of the building. This building spans the length of an entire block and is a quarter of a block in width. It's large enough that it had to be built over the alley to allow for vehicle access. I could exit in the alley if I wanted to.

Dylan hands me the note with two pieces of tape in the corners for me to stick it to the windows. I chuckle when I see she colored it all in. Outlined in black Sharpie are letters colored in red that look like blood.

"Nice touch."

She smiles and giggles. "Thank you. I thought he'd appreciate that."

I grin. "Just hang onto it until we get word from Josh. We'll likely be escorted down by our guards or Josh himself."

"VIP treatment."

I laugh. "Yes. Just the way I know you like it." I glance at her as she blushes and smiles even wider. "Man, I don't know what his fucking game is. He has to know I'd call him in."

"Maybe he's super cocky."

I shake my head. "Nah. I think he has an escape plan."

"Well, the police would cover all doors, right?"

"Maybe not the police, but the police working with the mafia would. He has to know Josh and Ryan own the department. At least, that's what he'd think. Really, they just work closely together and have ways of making things happen, but this is just off." I watch dark SUVs pulling up around the hotel. Ironically, Ethan doesn't move. He watches them as I am. "What the fuck?" I whisper.

"What?"

"Well, the mafia is rolling up on the hotel right now. Ethan is just standing there."

"That doesn't make sense."

"Nope. It doesn't." His smile is cocky, but he makes no attempt to move. I put the note up in the window and watch for a little while until squad cars start showing up. He looks towards the penthouse once more. I know he sees the note because he gives one more cocky smile before he moves away from the window. "I don't fucking get it."

"What's happening?"

"Squads showed up. Everyone is moving into the hotel now, and he's chosen this moment to leave."

Dylan is quiet for a few moments. "What... about... the roof? Could he escape from there?"

"He'd still have to come down somehow. Fire escape. He could hide up there until they leave. It's a good vantage point, but the -" With as much force as a bullet, it hits me. I watch cops enter the penthouse with their guns drawn, but my eyes are on the roof. "Fuck!" I grab my phone and dial DJ. "Please pick up!"

Dylan looks at me with fear in her eyes. "Cole?"

"Pick up!" I yell into the phone.

"Kinda busy, Westwood," DJ answers. "They -"

"He's on the roof!" I practically yell.

"Can you see him? Where?"

"I don't know, DJ! The roof! But I don't know where anyone in that room went! No one came out of the entrance!"

"Hey! You six! With me!" DJ barks. I hear DJ running. I keep my eyes on the roof.

"Oh my God," Dylan says, stepping in front of me. "Helicopter. It has to be a helicopter!"

I curse that I can't see the roof from here. I'm tempted to sprint up to the roof, but I know better. Leaving Dylan alone would be a mistake. Me going up there alone sets me up to be shot. All I can do is hope they get there before he takes off.

I hear whirring coming from DJ's phone. "Stop! Stop right now! On the ground!" DJ commands. "On the ground!" I hear what sounds like the phone being dropped before I hear more yelling. Only further away this time. "On the ground!"

Shooting.

"Oh fuck."

"Cole!" Dylan screams.

I pull her close. "Shh, baby."

She wraps her arms around me as chaos ensues. I keep my eyes on the roof hoping for any kind of sign that everyone is okay. Dylan's body trembles. I glance only briefly at Josh and Gavin when they come in with guards behind them because all of my attention is focused completely on the helicopter that's lifting off the roof.

I hurry to switch my phone to video mode as I record it taking off. My hope is that Lance can use it to get any kind of identifying marks from it that can be used to tell us where he is.

"Let me guess," Josh growls. "Fucker got away."

"Yeah, but not without shooting," I respond. "And I got a video of the helicopter. I should've fucking known that was going to be his out."

"Don't beat yourself up for that," Gavin says. "No way any of us would know he'd use a helicopter. It's not the style of any biker gang I've ever heard of."

"He's smart. We need to stop underestimating him and think like Matthew would. He was obviously trained by him." When I can't see the helicopter anymore, I shut the camera off and see I'm still connected with DJ. I can still hear a lot of scuffling and yelling.

"Son of a bitch!" someone yells. "That was our chance!"

"We're not falling apart now! Back to headquarters to figure out where that asshole is going! Move!" DJ commands. I hear what sounds like the phone being picked up. "Fuck. I'm going to have to explain this shattered screen to Lyric now."

"That might be worse than losing Ethan," I joke.

"She's gonna kick my ass before she hugs me, thankful that I'm alive. That's not a conversation I want to have with her. Obviously, you saw he got away."

"Yep. I have it recorded."

"Good. Because it was a rental. I saw a rental tag, but couldn't see the company. Send me the video."

"Already on it. Sending it to Lance, too."

"Thanks." DJ hangs up, and I turn to Josh.

"Ready to go home? I just got news you're cleared. I was going to call before you called me." Josh and Gavin start picking up our bags.

"Yeah. Ready to get the hell out of here," I say. Keeping an arm around Dylan, I guide her out of the penthouse behind Josh and Gavin.

I know the backlash that's going to come as soon as the Superintendent does a press conference. People are going to be pissed. Unless we come out with everything we found, the city isn't going to be on my side. We need to find a way to turn their attention towards the real culprit.

Ethan Fucking Lucinio.

Chapter Eleven

🍎 Dylan 🍎

(One Week Later)

I finish off my routine with a perfect tumble and right punch up. The judges nod and start marking things down on the paper in front of them.

"Thank you, Ms. Remington. You'll be hearing from us either way soon," one of the guys on the team says before he focuses on his own paper.

I give a winning smile. "Thank you so much for having me!" I jog off the football field at Kingston University with that smile plastered on my face, but inside, my heart is beating out of control. My stomach is in knots. I'm going over every single move of my routine and critiquing it.

"Hey, princess. You did incredible out there," Cole says as he wraps his arms around me.

I hug him. "I don't exactly feel too confident. I landed my handspring with a foot slightly to the side. I don't think my arms were straight enough on the back handspring. I don't feel like my stomach was tucked enough. I think my posture was horrible, and my toe touch was something I never should've done." I burrow my face into his chest. I love the way he smells. So masculine but calming. Fresh but strong.

He kisses my neck and hugs me tighter as he sways gently with me. "Personally, I think all of that looked flawless. I didn't see a single mistake. You're being way too hard on yourself, baby."

I smile into his chest. "You're biased."

He chuckles. "Maybe a little, but I do know my cheerleaders." He grins teasingly against my neck, and I push him with a giggle. "Being serious, you are being very hard on yourself."

I sigh and pull away but play with the hem of his t-shirt and watch myself doing it. "I know, I guess, but until I get the call, I'm not sure I'll really believe it."

Cole tilts my chin up. "Listen to me. No matter what they choose, you were fucking amazing out there. Don't pick apart a performance like that. You know you did amazing. You know damn well that if they don't pick you, it's not on you. It's on them. They're the ones who fucked up. You have to look at all of your accomplishments. You showed them what a great asset you are to the team. They've seen everything you've done." He leans in and kisses me. When he pulls back, he's smiling. "Don't beat yourself down. What I saw was a hell of a tryout. You're levels above everyone else we saw. You know that."

I nod and take a deep breath. "You're right."

"I usually am." A cocky grin slides over his face.

I giggle. "And cocky."

He leans in and whispers in my ear, "You love my cock."

I laugh and swat his arm. "Stop!" I whisper-scream at him, looking around. He's grinning from ear to ear as he takes my hand. We turn to walk to his truck when a guard heads towards us.

"The press conference is starting soon, sir. The Superintendent would like you to be there when the evidence clearing you is presented."

"Thank you, Ben," Cole says. Cole leads me towards his truck.

"Sir, one more thing. Mr. Lucinio would like Dylan back at the compound."

Cole sighs and pauses. "Tell Josh I said no. She's got enough guards on her, including her personal one. I want her with me."

The guard grins. "No, sir. I'm not relaying that message to him. He's in a bad enough mood, and I'm choosing my life."

I can't help but giggle as Cole grins and shakes his head. "It's okay." I kiss his arm. "I can watch you on TV with Rosie and Dallas."

He looks down at me, mischief in his eyes. "You sure? I'm looking for a fight."

I laugh. "No fighting with Josh. Not that I don't think you could take him, but Dallas loves him, and I kinda like him a little bit."

Cole laughs as he starts walking again. "Thanks for the vote of confidence, but Josh might be the only one who has a chance of taking me. How about dinner later? We can celebrate you getting on the squad, because I know you will, and me getting my shield back."

"Oooh, I love that. Can dinner mean takeout and a movie? Because that sounds like the best date night ever."

He grins down at me. "How the hell did I get so lucky? A perfect date to you is a quiet night at home. You can't possibly be any more right for me."

I blush. "I've never been big on parties or going out. I did them with my cousins just to keep up reputation, but even they knew I'd prefer to just be in, or just hanging out with them. I loved the days we just barbecued and hit the pool."

When we get to his truck, he takes me in his arms and hugs me. "We can have as many of those days as you want."

How about forever? I think to myself. "I'd love that," I whisper to him.

Cole smiles and kisses me. I love the taste of him. I love the feel of him. I love all of him. I hate when he releases me. I hate even more being away from him, but I follow Ben and Landon, my new personal bodyguard, to Ben's SUV. I was pretty excited to learn that not only did Landon want to become a guard, but that he was assigned to me. We've become really good friends since. I know I wouldn't be here if I hadn't gotten into his car. I'm sure no one else would've done what he did.

"How do you think you did?" Landon asks after we're all in.

"I started picking apart everything the second I was done. Cole said he thinks I did really well, though. I hope I did."

"I think you did a good job, ma'am," Ben says as he starts pulling out of the parking lot.

I watch Cole drive in the opposite direction towards the police Headquarters building. I smile softly when we turn and I can't see him anymore. "Thank you, Ben."

"I don't know much about cheerleading, but you looked just as good as the cheerleaders that were cheering when I was in school," Landon says. "I don't think you'll have an issue getting on the squad."

"I just can't believe I made tryouts. Doing it on the field was truly a rush. I don't know how Josh managed to make the university reschedule."

Ben chuckles. "I'm pretty sure it came with a hefty price and a promise of his first born."

I laugh because I can't help it. "That would make me feel a little bad. The first born part. Josh is super well to do, from what I hear."

"He definitely has the money and doesn't mind spending it for a good cause. For never going to college, he's a smart businessman. I don't know if it's true, but someone told me he makes like two million a day with all of his businesses."

"Wow, that's a lot," Landon says. "No wonder he does so much charity work and stuff for the kids. I went to something he puts on every summer for the kids once. He donates a ton of money so kids here have stuff to do. I hear he even donated something to public schools and the inner city ones."

I can't help but be proud of someone like that, but I'm even more proud that I know him personally. That I get to be associated with a person who does so much for people and the community without a second thought. Someone so kind deserves so much recognition that Josh simply doesn't get. I'm pretty sure it's because he doesn't want it, though.

When we pull into the Crane and Lucinio complex, I perk up. Everyone's houses are so beautiful and exquisite in their own rights. They're all beautiful. None are the same. The drive down the road is one of my favorite things. I love seeing all of the beauty.

Ben pulls into Josh's driveway, and he and Landon step out. I've learned quickly that I'm not allowed to get out first. Given I have a target on my head, they get out first and make sure it's safe for me. Once they do, Landon opens my door, and I'm escorted wherever I'm going. Usually Cole is with me, but Landon is never far away.

When we get to the door, Dallas opens it and greets me with a hug as she pulls me inside. "Josh is with Cole at Headquarters, but the press conference is about to start."

I nervously follow. "I wonder what's going to happen." I sit down between her and Rosie as Dallas turns the TV up and hands me a flavored water bottle. I take it.

"Mostly, they're just going over the evidence that proves it's not him." Rosie tells me.

"That makes me feel better," I say, taking a drink. "Thank God for Lance."

"I've said that so many times," Dallas says with a laugh. Our attention all falls to the TV when the Superintendent of Police stands at the podium.

"Ladies and Gentleman. I've gathered you here today to address a problem that has been blown very much out of proportion by the media. Recently, one of our Sergeants in our Major Crimes unit was accused of horribly and viciously murdering a man in unadulterated cold blood. Our department was investigating internally, but with the scrutiny on us, we outsourced the investigation to an independent investigator and the Bureau of Criminal Apprehension, also known as the BCA. The investigation concluded recently. This press conference is for transparency purposes where I will share the findings with you and the citizens of our great city."

Dallas giggles as the Superintendent flips a page in his notes. "Independent investigator from the mafia."

Rosie and I laugh as the Superintendent starts speaking again. "I have included a packet for each of you today. If you'll flip to page one, you'll see the details of the incident. The second page and several pages after shows crime scene images that may not be suitable for all audiences. You may choose to show them on your broadcasts or not. On page thirty-one, you'll find the beginnings of the findings of the report from our independent investigator. The highlighted sections are the important pieces that I'll go over now. Specifically, I'd like to draw your attention to the third highlighted area that discusses the video itself being staged and edited. The investigator lists several areas of the video that are problematic and gives numerous reasons why each of these sections are problems."

We watch intensely as he goes through each area. By the time he's finished, it's so obvious the video is fake that the idea anyone believed it in the first place is unbelievable. When he moves onto how the BCA's findings were all very much in sync with the independent investigator, I can't help but laugh out loud.

"Cole Westwood, the Sergeant publicly identified as the person in this video, has been villainized by the media and the public in such a heinous manner that apologies are never going to suffice. There was a riot in this city because of the irresponsible behavior on a national level by the media. The person in this video remains unidentified. We are still trying to strip the layers of Artificial Intelligence programs used to create the face of the person in this video. The Chicago Police Department is actively attempting to do this through several programs we have access to as well as with help from FBI contacts. To conclude, Sergeant Westwood was and still is an active member of Chicago Police Department. While he was put on administrative leave for the duration of this investigation, he is back to full duty with the department's apologies. You'll also find information in your packets regarding the warrant that was filed falsely in his arrest. The deputy who created it doesn't exist, and the judge who signed it is deceased and has been for several years. Had the department had the time and resources to investigate this before the media's involvement, this investigation would've concluded long ago. I have nothing further to say. No questions."

The Superintendent moves away from the podium. The camera zooms out to show the entire room. Several reporters are seated and yelling questions. There are other people on the stage, including someone I think is the Mayor.

But it's the side of the stage where my eyes land. The left side of it where Cole is standing next to a pretty blond who is not just hugging him, but kissing him, too. Not the cheek. Not a kiss of congratulations. No. Nothing like that. The blond with the curves any woman would die for has her tongue down Cole's throat. The man who I thought was my boyfriend. His hands grip her hips just like they do mine as the camera cuts to someone in the newsroom telling us there we all have it and concluding the press conference.

My stomach clenches. My heart drops. Tears sting my eyes. I blink them away and swallow over the lump in my throat. I put a hand up to my mouth and wrap the other around my middle.

"Oh my God," Rosie whispers.

Dallas shakes her head in disbelief. "There... has to be some kind of explanation."

"There has to be, Dylan," Rosie agrees. "There has to be. That's not Cole. Not the Cole we know."

I can't speak. Breathing isn't coming naturally. My body rejects air completely. My chest is so tight that it forces my body to follow suit.

I sniffle. "Can I stay with one of you?" I whisper.

"Of course," Rosie says as they both hug me. "You don't even have to ask. Of course you can." She looks up at Dallas. "Right?"

Dallas nods. "We'll make it work. It'll be okay."

I take a breath. "I need to get my stuff. I don't have much, but it's all at Cole's. He gave me the way to get in." I nod as my plan falls into place. "I'll have Landon help me."

I hurry out of the house calling him, having enough sense to not just run to his house without someone with me, just in case, I wait for Landon to pull up in one of the Lucinio Mafia's SUVs. We drive in silence to Cole's house, and I jump out before he lets me.

"Jesus. Dylan, wait!" Landon runs after me grabbing my arm as he hurries me to the house and looks around. "Hurry up and get in."

I do as he asks. I run upstairs to Cole's room and start grabbing my stuff. "Can you just start putting this stuff in my bags?" I put them on the bed.

"What the hell is going on, Dylan?"

"I just can't be here. That's all. My heart can't handle it."

"Are you talking about what everyone saw on TV with Cole? Because I think there's a whole story behind that."

"Please just put stuff in the bags." I'm doing all I can to fight the tears.

I hear Landon sigh, but I don't pay attention. I don't know when Cole will be back, and I don't want to risk seeing him. I know what I saw, and it didn't look innocent. I need time to think, and right now all I can think about is a beautiful girl's tongue down his throat right after he promised me a perfect date. Right after I was thinking of forever.

It was stupid. It's all stupid. Why would I possibly think of that with a man who I started out hating just as much as he hated me? It hasn't even been a month. How could I let myself fall for Cole's charms when it's so obvious the type of man he is as a person? He's cocky. Arrogant. He's the literal devil in a nice looking package. Those angel wings on his back are anything but angelic.

When I finish getting all of my stuff packed, I hurry Landon down the stairs. We're almost to the door when Cole walks in. My heart, once again, stops beating at the very sight of him. He takes my breath away. He's the only man who made me feel worthy of the nickname princess. The only one who didn't make me feel like it was as derogatory as everyone else made it.

He furrows his eyebrows in confusion as Landon walks out of the house with my bags as he shakes his head. Cole looks at me. "What's going on? You okay? What happened?" He reaches for me.

I step back, just out of his reach and wrap my arms around myself as I look down. I can't make eye contact. It'll break me into a million pieces. "I'm… staying with Rosie for a little while," I whisper.

"What? Why? What happened?"

His words snap something inside me. I look up at him with a glare. "Like you don't know?" I push past him and run out the door.

He stands in the middle of the room in shock briefly before he moves, but I'm already in the SUV. I lock the door when I see him charging after me. "Dylan! What the fuck is happening? Talk to me!"

Landon sighs as he backs out of the driveway. "Maybe you should talk to him."

"I will. I just can't right now, Landon." I shake my head. I can't.

I'm too broken. Shattered. Stupid for thinking I was good enough for a man like him.

It's not a long drive. When we get to Rosie's, she and Dallas are standing outside waiting for me. It's not until we're inside in Rosie's room that I let myself truly succumb to the implosion of my heart.

Chapter Twelve

☙ Cole ☙

I watch the tail lights until they turn into Lance's and Damon's driveway. I turn back into my house and close the door when Dylan hurries into the house with Rosie and Dallas.

"What the fuck?" I ask myself, still completely confused about what the hell is going on. I sit on my couch and rub my temples.

I thought everything was going fine. Her tryout looked fucking fantastic. She didn't see the faces of the cheerleaders judging her. They were all smiles. They were commenting on particular moves and nodding to each other. When she did a move that looked complicated as fuck to me, the guy in the middle actually just about applauded, but he held back and did a silent 'yeah' motion instead. I didn't want to tell her any of that because I didn't want to get her hopes up in the unlikely event she isn't picked for the team.

Everything was perfect then. She was nervous but happy. She melted into my touch. She purred into my kiss. It was all good.

So, what the fuck happened between then and now? What made her decide to just fucking leave without saying anything to me? We were getting along very well. She's been staying here since we left the penthouse, and we've gotten considerably closer.

I turn on the evening news and toss the remote on the couch as I head for the kitchen to get a drink. I pull a bottle of Michelob out of the fridge and pop the top using the edge of the counter. I take a long drink. I'm not one to drink much, but sometimes, I like a cold one or two. My eyes fall on the TV. Carmella is plastered in the center of it with her tongue down my throat and my hands on her hips before the camera cuts.

"You've got to be fucking kidding me," I say with a sudden sick feeling.

"Oh, we've been together for a little over a year," Carmella says behind the anchor desk as someone asks her questions. "Obviously, during this controversy, we haven't been able to talk or be together because I've had to remain unbiased in my reporting, but I'd never stopped believing in his innocence. Cole is a truly incredible person. I knew in my heart he couldn't have done such a horrible thing."

"How was he during all of this?" the guy interviewing her asks.

"Oh, distraught for sure. He loves his job. This was an awful thing to happen."

"The department is coming down on us pretty hard for reporting false information. You were a big part of that. Is he understanding and forgiving towards you?"

"Jesus Christ." I down the bottle in the next long drink.

"Oh, for sure. He knew I had a job to do. It was hard for the both of us, but I had to go with the information we all had."

I shake my head. "Yeah. Right. You walked when I needed you the most. Good thing I never loved you and just liked the fuck. And now, you've successfully ruined the one relationship I actually give a fuck about."

I tune her out when she starts talking again. I walk to the couch and grab the remote again as I sit down. I shut the TV off and see Dylan's sketchbook on the table. In her rush to leave, she must've forgotten it.

I reach for it and stare at the cover. Like I've wanted to do ever since she started using it, I want to take a peek, but I don't. I let out a breath. For years, I've admittedly been a self-centered prick. I know it as well as everyone else does. Ever since a serious relationship I had when I was younger ended in the most bitter ending imaginable, I've steered clear

94

from falling in love again. She wrecked me. It wasn't until Dylan came in my life that I truly started believing there might be a chance for me after all.

I also know very well how self-destructive I am. When things are going well in my life, I find a way to fuck it up somehow. The longest relationship I've had since the woman I honestly thought I'd spend my life with was Carmella. It was never really a relationship, though. I saw it clear as day when she told me she wanted to break up until things blew over. Everything I wanted to deny was right there, front and center, just waiting for me to see.

I run my thumb over the pages of the sketchbook before making a decision. I pick up the drawing pencils I bought her and stand. Enough living my life this way. I'm not letting her go. I'm going to fight for her. She, at the very least, needs to hear me out. I'm not the villain she believes me to be. She needs to hear the truth from me and me alone. I didn't kiss Carmella. She threw her arms around me and kissed me. I was fucking surprised, but once I got my bearings back, I gripped her hips and pushed her away. I told her we were done.

I glare at the TV that's now off. I'll deal with her later. Dylan is more important to me than her and whatever the fuck game of manipulation she's playing. I stride to my door with purpose and close it behind me after I walk out. I make my way to Damon's and Lance's. It's only a few houses away, so getting there takes no time.

It's what I see when I get there that ties me in knots.

"We'll get through it. I'm here for you, okay?" Landon says as he takes *my girl* in his arms.

Dylan wraps her arms around his neck and presses closer. Just like she does with me. "Thank you, Landon. You're really the best."

I swallow hard, feeling like I've been roundhouse kicked in the fucking stomach. Instead of letting her see that pain, though, I look at it like an eye for an eye. She saw another woman kissing me, so why not let me see her willingly this close to another man. It's not until Landon kisses her, on the cheek, but it's enough for me, that I lose all composure.

I slam her sketchbook and pencils on top of the SUV. "I get it now. Makes perfect sense." I turn on my heel and march my way back to my house.

"Cole! It's not what you fucking think, man!" Landon yells after me, but I don't stop.

Not what I fucking think? I was right to be jealous of the two of them this whole time. The way she talked about him. How happy she got when she got a text from him. The way she got giddy when she saw him. I wasn't too fucking fond of Josh's decision to put him as her personal bodyguard, but I trust him enough to trust his judgement.

I can't deny the kid did a good job getting her out of trouble, then getting out of it himself. It still doesn't mean I like the fact that Josh not only hired him as a guard, but then put him on her personal security detail. I didn't trust Landon's skills then, and I sure as fuck don't now, but it's always been more than that. I don't fucking trust him. I'm sure he's a great guy and very trustworthy, but I knew fuck well I couldn't trust him with her. The proof is in what I just saw. That wasn't just a friendly hug and kiss. I know when guys like him are trying to win someone over. I fucking *was* him.

It was different when Dylan was around. She made me want to be better, and I think I was, but maybe people never change. Maybe I'm always going to be the arrogant, unfixable asshole. The one who burns bridges just as quickly as relationships.

I enter my house and slam the door behind me. I spend several moments pacing and trying to work off steam, but in the end, I find myself in my whiskey cabinet searching for my best bottle. William Larue Weller Bourbon Whiskey. I was saving it for a special occasion, but this seems like a more appropriate time.

Foregoing a shot glass, I sit at the kitchen table with another beer as my chaser. The more I drink, the hazier Dylan's face should become, but it doesn't work that way. Halfway into the bottle, her beautiful features are sharper than ever. I can feel her hair against my chest while I hold her close at night. I can see her submissive eyes wide with wonder and lust as she rides me. It's only been a couple of weeks, but we've built a connection I honestly didn't believe could be severed so quickly.

All because my fucking ex had to get some wild hair up her ass and kissed me in front of the damn cameras. I don't know what the fuck she was thinking, but the fact that Dylan fell for it hook, line, and sinker pisses me off. It makes me wonder just how smart she really is.

Considering the way she was hugging her fucking bodyguard, maybe I'm the stupid one for falling for her in the first place.

Admitting I feel for her hurts a lot worse than seeing her in that embrace. Him swaying with her like that. Her hugging him the way she does me. It all fucks with my mind, but it's my heart that takes the brunt of the onslaught coming at me.

It's my all out anger that has me texting Carmella as I finish off my bottle of beer. I grab a new one after telling her to get her ass over her. I text the guards at the gate to let her through because I know the moment we broke up, she would've been put on a list to keep her out, but I need to talk to her. I need to figure out what the fuck her plan is.

As I wait for her, I finish off the bottle of whiskey and the beer. I can feel the effects, but I'm too pissed off to care. Who the fuck cares if I'm a little dizzy? I'm still thinking clearly. Too clearly. Clearly enough to grab another bottle of beer and decide to sip it instead of down it. Clearly enough to take my empty bottle of whiskey and bring it to the couch so I can swallow the last fucking drop.

I don't know how much time passes before Carmella finally knocks on the door, but it's enough for me to get through four more bottles. I've lost count how many I've had, but it's not enough if I can still see Dylan's face and sexy body.

I open the door, stumbling as I take a step back to let Carmella in. "Fushing sminally," I growl.

She's wearing a short as hell black skirt to match her teal shirt that somehow ties in the back. The black stilettos that used to make my mouth water for her toned legs wrapped around my shoulders as I drilled her just make me sick now.

"I'm here, baby. What did you want to talk about?"

I close the door and stumble against it. I drop my now empty bottle that I was holding and shake my head, but it just makes me more unstable. "Fush," I whisper.

"Cole? What's wrong? Are you okay? How much did you drink?"

I fight back some nausea with my eyes closed when I feel her wrap herself around me. "'m fin." I turn slowly towards her and lean against the door. "Wha' th' fush were you sink' kishing me today?"

"Cole, we were just on a break until this blew over. You know that. It's over." She presses against me, tucking her fingertips in the waistband of my jeans.

I push her back. "Gerroff, C'r'ella. 're dom. I tol' shu it was ov'r," I slur.

She pouts and pushes some hair behind her ear. "It doesn't feel like it. You still want me." She looks pointedly down at my dick.

My eyes follow hers. "Fush aw th' way osh. 'm nosh hard. Shu know 'm jus' big."

"We could always fix that." She slithers like a snake up to me and quickly undoes my belt, but I push her back again.

"Knock osh, C'r'ella." I take a chance and push myself off the door using the wall for balance. "'re nosh back toge'er. Shoo sh'lf oot." Once I reach the end of the wall, I try walking on my own, but it fails epically. I drop like a sack of bricks face first to the floor.

"Oh my God! Cole!" Carmella kneels next to me. "How much did you drink? Jesus. It smells like a brewery in here."

"Too mush," I mumble with my cheek against the carpet, finally admitting that I drank way too fucking much. My eyes close, and I groan. I feel Carmella trying to help me up. "G'sh osh."

"Cole, come on. The least we can do is get you to bed."

I hate to admit she's right, so after a few moments of her pulling on my arm, I finally help her as much as I can. Using the end table and chair, I pull myself up enough for her to get her body underneath me.

Using her strength and body weight to support me, even though she's half my weight, she manages to get me standing. She fights to get me up the stairs, but she's out of breath halfway up, and we both fall.

"Fush," I rumble as I roll off her.

"Almost there, baby," she croons.

"Shup c'll'ng me b'by." I lay on my back with my eyes closed and feel the darkness of passing out creeping up on me. "Too mush...," I murmur. My head is starting to pound, and that sick feeling is coming back.

"Come on, Cole. We're almost there. Can you use the railing?"

My eyes snap open, and I get dizzy again. I groan because whatever is against my back actually hurts. It takes me a few moments to reorient myself enough to realize I'm still on the stairs. Carmella is standing above me and tugging on me until she gets me to a sitting position. I feel like the world is spinning upside down.

"Fuf," I growl.

"Can you crawl? Please?"

I look to the side of me and see the stairs. I start turning, nearly knocking Carmella down the stairs. I hear her murmuring something, but I don't really hear her. I crawl up the stairs slowly, but it feels like lightning to me.

Once I reach the top, I become determined to at least get to my bed. I'll never tell her, but I'm grateful Carmella helps me to stand.

"I'll hu stha wash," I slur. I can't even understand what I'm saying, so I don't know how I expect her to.

"I got you, babe." She slings her arm around my waist and my arm over her shoulder.

Somehow, she gets me to bed and helps me sit down. While she keeps me sitting up, she turns down the blankets and manages to get my shirt off.

"'Nuff." I swat my hand to shoo her away. My vision is getting a lot more blurry, and my head feels like it's going to explode. I manage to lay down, but just before I pass out completely, she's back.

She moves me onto my back and straddles me. I can barely see anything, but I can make out that she's naked. "You can stay up a little while, can't you?" Her hand moves down my abs until they're on my button and zipper. She gets my button undone and zipper down before I can react.

"Osh."

"Come on, Cole. You can do it, baby."

"'Nuff, 'M'lla."

With the last bit of strength and sense I have left, I turn to my side and push her off me onto the bed. I'm not gonna last any longer. I feel the bile rising. She's saying something, but I don't know what it is. I vaguely feel myself move my leg enough so I'm not totally on my stomach before a blissful darkness takes over and I fall into a dreamless sleep.

Chapter Thirteen

☙ Dylan ☙

I finish getting dressed and glance at my clock. It's 4:30am. Cole should just be getting up and heading to his gym. He's a creature of habit. He wakes up every morning at this exact time. He goes to the bathroom and brushes his teeth. Then, he goes to his kitchen and makes a protein shake, which he carries to the gym with him. He starts his workout on the treadmill as a warm up as he drinks the shake. Once he's finished, he starts the rest of his workout. If I time it right and leave right now, I'll make it to his house just as he's heading for the gym.

I let out a breath as I start putting up my hair in a messy bun while I'm walking down the stairs of Rosie's house. I feel awful about yesterday. Landon and Rosie were able to really talk me down and help me realize that just because what I saw looked bad, it might not have been all as it seemed. Dallas even told me that she never liked Carmella and always had a bad feeling about her.

I didn't sleep at all. The only thing I could think of is Cole's face when he saw me hugging Landon. He knows we've become friends, but he has no idea that Landon is gay. If I were him and saw me hugging another guy that he knows I'm close to, I'd feel like I'd just been punched. I felt exactly that when I saw Carmella all over him. It made everything worse to see her being interviewed about him later and calling herself his girlfriend.

I owe it to Cole to at least explain what happened. Just as he owes it to me to tell him that what he saw was nothing more than a friend hugging another friend to comfort her after she realized what an idiot she'd been. I wanted to chase him, but Landon stopped me. He said it would be better to let us both calm down before we talked. After thinking things through, I realized he was right. It gave me an opportunity to plan what I want to say to him, especially since I know he'll revert right back to his conceited dickhead ways. It's his defense mechanism for whatever happened to him when he was younger and dating a woman he thought he was really in love with.

So, when I leave the house and close the door quietly behind me, I briskly walk to Cole's house with purpose. I'm not supposed to go anywhere without security. Usually, I'd listen to that, but getting to Cole is too important to me to wait for anyone.

I tilt my head when I see a car I don't recognize in his driveaway, but it's not really even that one that concerns me. Dane's truck is there, but so is Nick Crane's and Taylor Reddick's. Both of them work with Cole. It's his first day back today, but it seems odd that all three of them are there. I suddenly get a very bad feeling and start walking faster.

Like I'm on a rollercoaster, my heart drops into the pit of my stomach when Dane's truck suddenly backs out of the driveway with lights and sirens activated.

"Oh my God." Alarmed, I start running, slowing when I see Dane driving his truck, Carmella in the passenger's seat, and Dr. Freeman in the back with his eyes focused down. It looks like he's working on someone.

At that moment, Taylor backs out of the driveway with his lights and sirens activated. He speeds past Dane, taking the lead, and the two of them begin driving even faster. My heart, definitely relocated at this point, starts beating faster, I begin hyperventilating as I freeze in place and watch them drive off.

"Get in!" Josh barks, snapping me out of the confused haze I'm fighting. I hadn't even noticed that Nick had pulled out of Cole's driveway and stopped in front of where I'm standing.

I quickly do as he says the moment the back door to Nick's truck flies open. I barely have the door closed when Nick activates his lights and sirens and takes off after Dane and Taylor.

Fighting to breathe, I pull my hoodie over my mouth and nose and close my eyes. "Wh-what's h-happening?" I breathe in and count slowly to five before breathing out.

"I don't know, sweetheart," Nick says. "I got a call from Dane to get to Cole's house. By the time I got there, Josh and Dane were carrying Cole to Dane's truck."

I keep my eyes closed and try to focus on steady breathing, but it's not the easiest task to complete over the sobs suddenly wracking my body. My brain, still somehow logical and trying to gain control of the rest of me, is screaming at Josh to pick up on Nick's subtle hint and explain just what in the hell is going on. Fill in the blanks.

"I don't know, Dylan. I suspect, but I don't know. I got a call from Dane to get the doctor. So, I did and met him there. Dane was screaming at Carmella and trying to wake Cole up. Doc showed up, and we moved fast, but it looks like alcohol poisoning, sweetheart."

Carmella.

Alcohol poisoning.

Not waking up.

Carmella.

Alcohol poisoning.

Not waking up.

The words repeat in my head and play over and over and over again just like my favorite song. Only it's not a song. It's not my favorite. And it doesn't make me happy.

Well, I knew he would revert to his asshole ways to lash out. And boy did he ever.

I shake my head to rid those thoughts, but they creep in anyway. What was Carmella doing there? Did she just show up? Was he drunk before she came? Did he invite her over and they drank together? Was he drinking and then invite her? Did they fuck?

All of the images that puts in my mind make the breathing quicken all over again, so I tuck myself back in my hoodie and put my hood up. I close my eyes, but they open on their own when I start thinking of the two of them embracing; kissing the way he kisses me.

Fucking.

I start partially coughing and partially gagging. The sobs are back, and I choke on them, making it all worse.

"Breathe in the fresh air, honey," Nick says.

I feel cool air against me. I quickly put my hood down and pop out of my hoodie. I practically stick my head out the window that he put down as I gulp in mouthfuls of air, but it's not enough. It doesn't reach my lungs. My chest feels like it's collapsing. My entire upper body feels numb. Am I having a heart attack?

I rub my chest. It suddenly feels like it's on fire. I can hear my heartbeat in my ears. My breathing becomes more and more erratic. I jump when I feel a hand on my thigh and look down at it without really recognizing what it is.

"Dylan. Look at me."

My eyes snap to the owner of the commanding voice. "Wh-"

"Look at me." Josh. It's Josh. I can't quite catch up to myself. I feel like my entire body is running a marathon that I'm not involved in. "Dylan." His voice is the calm in tornadic wind, though still the command that I need in order to follow him to safety. "You need to breathe. Focus on me. Breathe. What color are my eyes?"

"Bl-blue."

"That's good. Breathe." He takes a deep breath, and I follow his lead. "Bite the inside of your cheek."

I furrow my brows, but do as he says. I wince. "Ow…"

"Good. Tell me what you taste."

"U-um… skin… I think… Kind of like metal."

He nods. "Good. Breathe." He makes a show of taking a deep breath as he squeezes my knee. I don't know if he knows it, but he centers me. I didn't realize it, but I'm digging my nails into my own palms. I take another deep breath with him as I slowly unclench my fists. "Tell me what you feel."

I let out the breath and feel my heart rhythm slowly return to normal, though it's still far from in my control. "Pain. In my chest. My hands from where my nails were digging." I grab his hand that's on my knee. Still keeping the connection I need, he moves his hand so it's palm up. He grasps my hand.

"Breathe." He takes another slow, calming breath, not breaking eye contact with me. I follow his breathing and nod. "Tell me what you hear."

"The wind. The sirens."

"Good. You're doing so good. I'm very proud of you. Breathe." Once more he takes a deep breath. I mimic him, letting out just as slowly as he does. "What do you smell?"

"The city. I smell the city."

"Good. That's good. One more time. Breathe." He takes one more breath. I follow, letting it out just as slowly as him. Feeling is starting to come back to my body. I can't hear my heartbeat in my ears anymore. It's calmed significantly. My chest isn't on fire anymore. "We're almost to the hospital, okay? We'll know a lot more when we get there." Josh squeezes my hand as I nod.

"Please just promise me he'll be okay. Lie if you have to," I beg.

"I can't do that, sweetheart. You know me far better than that. I will promise you that everything, the best care, the best doctor, the best of everything is at Cole's disposal. If anyone can help him, it's the people who will be taking care of him. I promise that."

I close my eyes and nod, knowing that's all I'm getting. I open my eyes once we stop, and I hear a door open. I didn't notice, but we must've had guard's following us because there are a lot of people here, Landon included.

Landon is standing at my door. I turn and look at him, but I'm physically incapable of letting Josh's hand go. So much is going on around me that I can't focus on any one thing. Any one conversation. It's not until Landon takes my other hand in his that I'm finally able to release Josh. I practically fling myself at my bodyguard as he helps me out of Nick's truck. Landon hugs me.

"They took him in already. Dane is waiting for us. He sent Carmella to the waiting room," Taylor tells Josh.

"Good," Josh says. "Ben, get these vehicles parked."

"Yes, sir," Ben responds before he starts making commands to the other guards.

Some of the guards start parking vehicles while others stick with us. We all follow Josh's lead as we walk into the hospital. Landon sticks next to me like glue. I know it's his job, but it's also a great comfort to me to have a friend here during this.

"Access to the private waiting room in the private wing," Dane says, handing out passes. "We have the room to ourselves. There's two more up there for others, but Cole will be the only one up there right now anyway. They just discharged some basketball star."

"Good," Josh nods as Dane finishes handing out passes.

I can see how worried he is. I know Dane is Cole's best friend, and vice versa, but all the families who live on the compound are like family to him. Cole didn't open up much to me over the past few weeks, but he did say that he didn't have the best childhood. His dad was a cop who was killed in the line of duty in Los Angeles. The number under his tattoo is what his dad's badge number was. His mom couldn't afford to keep up and killed herself when Cole was a teenager. He was put into the system. Despite everything, he stayed a good kid. He kept preserving and following his dreams. He made a life for himself. He had his own house when most people his age were still figuring things out.

I stay quiet as I follow everyone to the private waiting room. People are on phones calling others. I just stick close to Josh's side as Landon stays close to me. I hug myself as tightly as I can and keep my head down. By the time we get to the waiting room, I'm already a mess again.

"What is *she* doing here?" an annoying voice that's more awful than nails on a chalkboard says. I'd, unfortunately, recognize it anywhere.

"I think the better question here is why are you?" Taylor growls from behind me. I'd jump, but I'm oddly comforted by both him and his tone. "She's his girlfriend. Didn't you guys break up?"

I look at Taylor a little curiously as he steps closer to me. Even more strange to me is all of the guys have sort of formed around me and are facing her down. The guards, including Landon, mill around the room, but Taylor, Dane, Nick, and Josh are all standing at my side. It makes me feel both brave and like someone really is with me in this whole thing.

"Well, you're all wrong. We got back together last night. He'd tell you, but obviously, he has bigger problems." She sniffles and turns away, but it's so obviously fake.

It doesn't matter, though. The damage is already done. Her words break my heart even more, even though I have no idea if they're true or not. If they are, then she was there for Cole when he spiraled. It's all my fault. I should've just talked to him instead of running away. They always say a person can't be hurt if they're the first to leave. Turns out that statement is inaccurate because the way I'm hurting right now. Even if they didn't get back together last night, she was still there for him when I should've been. It's something I'll never forgive myself for.

Instead of arguing, I just drop my head and let her words punch holes in my already damaged heart. I sit down in the corner of the room on a chair and curl into myself. After a brief argument between his brothers, though, not by blood, and Carmella, everything in the room becomes deathly quiet. Someone takes pity on me at some point and covers me with a blanket when they notice I'm shivering, but it doesn't ease the chills. These come from somewhere deep. Somewhere in my bones. I'm terrified at having no information on Cole.

While we wait for any news, no matter how little, the rest of the family begins trickling in. People from both the Crane family and Lucinio family fill the room. The longer we all wait, the more the tension in the room rises.

Finally, Dr. Freeman enters with a nurse and another doctor, an adorable older man with a cheery smile, even though it looks dimmed right now. I perk up and look at them with red-rimmed and dry eyes from the silent tears that overtook me the past few hours. I'm supposed to be strong, not cry, but crying is all I seem to be doing lately.

Josh stands, always the tough one in all of this. "Doc? How is he?"

"He's going to make it," Dr. Freeman says. A collective sigh of relief ripples through the room like a wave. "He's been through a lot, Josh."

"Okay, wait just a second," Raleigh says as she stands. She'd been talking to Lyric and Harleigh, two of the women in this family. Raleigh is Alex's wife. Harleigh is Gavin's. Lyric is Matt's and DJ's.

"This is a family matter," Lyric says, glaring right at Carmella. "No hussies." I'm sure that wouldn't have been as adorable if she didn't have a British accent.

"Lyric," DJ rumbles in warning.

"What?" she asks innocently, blinking down at him. I can't help but chuckle, but I'm nice enough to hide it behind blankets. DJ just shakes his head and grins as Lyric turns back to a shocked Carmella.

"That means get out," Harleigh says to Carmella.

"Excuse me? Cole is *my* boyfriend. What are you?" Carmella asks, standing her ground.

Harleigh puts a hand up to her chest. "His family. Which means I trump you. Now, leave."

"Not a chance!" Carmella shrieks. I wince at the sound that comes out of her mouth.

"Harleigh," Gavin warns. He takes her hand and tugs her back to him as he ushers the other two with him. "Let it go."

"She shouldn't be here," Lyric pouts.

"Agreed, but we aren't the ones making that call," Gavin says. "Cole is. When he wakes up."

"Can I continue now?" Dr. Freeman asks with a hint of a smile.

Josh chuckles. "Go ahead, doc."

"He had to get his stomach pumped. I don't know how he drank as much as he did, but from what I saw at his house, it was a lot." He turns to Carmella. "How much of what was there did you drink?"

"Nothing! When I got there, he was already so drunk he couldn't stand. He was slurring. It took me like thirty minutes to even get him to his bedroom."

Dr. Freeman just nods and looks back at the other doctor. "Then, my guess is probably pretty accurate, Dr. Chantau. I saw eight bottles and the bottle of whiskey. They were all empty."

Dr. Chantau nods as I gasp. It hurts me even deeper knowing he drank that much because of what I did to him. Because I didn't talk to him. "We'll need to keep him under for a little while while we get him rehydrated. He's not in any condition to be awake. He needs time to heal."

"Wait," I nearly whisper. Both doctors and the nurse look at me. "What... do you mean... keep him under?"

Dr. Chantau gives me a gentle smile. "It just means we've put him into a medically induced coma. He's okay. He's perfectly functional. We just have a breathing tube in him and we're slowly hydrating him. He's in a lot of pain from the stomach pump and the situation as a whole."

"Shouldn't you be telling me all of this? I'm his girlfriend. Not her." Carmella sniffles, and I silence myself.

But not Josh.

Ever the protector. "Carmella, do yourself a favor and shut the fuck up. I don't care if you're the fucking King of England. I will end you. No one will ever find you. Do you got me?"

She glares at him. "But he's not hers! He's -"

"My brother!" Josh booms. "That's what he is! Not your anything! He's my fucking family! Now, shut the hell up, or I swear to fuck, I'll shove you out of that window behind you, and no one will bat a fucking eye! Understand me?"

Carmella looks at him wide-eyed and nods with open-mouthed shock. "Y-yes."

"Yes what?" Josh barks.

Carmella jumps. "Sir. Y-yes, s-sir."

Josh gives her one more withering look and turns back to the doctors. I can't help but notice the nurse has taken a step back. "Tell me what we're doing, Eric," Josh says to Dr. Freeman. I've never heard his real name before, but Eric is fitting.

Eric clears his throat. "We wait. This is his nurse." He gestures to the nurse behind him. "Her name is Betty. She's going to stay on the whole time, of course taking breaks. She'll get sleep time because we'll all three be taking our shifts."

"Betty, it's nice to meet you." Josh extends his hand, but doesn't step forward. I instantly recognize the gesture because he's done that to me. He knows very well that he scares people. If he can sense that he's done something to make that happen, he'll let the person come to him. "I'm Josh."

Betty nods slowly and steps forward. She takes Josh's hand, and he gives it a gentle shake. "Nice to meet you. Um… I'll be on Cole's care team with the doctors. I'm a trauma nurse. I have thirty-one years of experience. He's in good hands."

"I appreciate that, ma'am. Thank you," Josh says.

"We're allowing one person back there with him," Eric says as he turns to me.

My eyes widen. "Oh, um…" Before I can respond, Carmella pipes up.

"That's obviously going to be me." She storms towards the door, but both doctors and the nurse block her path. She glares at them.

"It should be Dylan," Ryan Crane, a man I've only met a handful of times says as he stands for the first time. He takes his place next to Josh. "No one here knows what the hell happened last night, but none of us trust you're back together. Especially if he was so drunk, he got alcohol poisoning because of it." He narrows his eyes at her and crosses his arms over his chest. Every single person in the room agrees.

"Well, it's not up to you. It's not up to any of you," Carmella seethes. "I'm the one he called last night, and if you don't believe me, you can see the text." She takes her phone out of her pocket and starts scrolling through it before she holds it up. "See?"

"I don't care, Carmella," Josh says. "I'll go back there myself before I'll let you, but Ryan is right. It should be Dylan."

I shake my head. As painful as it is for me to say, I take a deep breath. "Let her go," I say as loudly as I can, though it's still barely above a whisper.

Josh looks at me. Carmella smirks. He walks to me and kneels in front of me. "You know I'm not letting her anywhere near that room if you tell me you want to be with him."

"I do," I whisper. "I do want to be with him. More than anything, Josh, but I don't know what we are. What if she's telling the truth? What if they really did get back together last night?"

"Then, I don't think it was a rational decision that he made while he was sober and thinking clearly."

"But you think," I whisper again. "You don't know."

My words seem to hit him, even though he doesn't want me to be right. Josh doesn't assume. Assumptions are what get people killed. He doesn't know. He shakes his head as he stands.

"Fine. I'll let you go, but I'm going to warn you, Carmella." Josh moves closer to her and stands over her. She shrinks. "If you fuck anything up, I'm coming for you."

Carmella nods and hurries from the room as I snuggle back down into my blankets. I feel like a microwaved tragedy, but I know when I've lost.

I just didn't expect to lose so fast.

Chapter Fourteen

❦ Cole ❦

(Two Days Later)

"Dylan?" I call out in the dark forest I'm wandering through. It's been hours, but I'm not giving up. She's coming home with me. I saw her walking out here. I hear her voice whispering to me, but I can't find her.

The brush I'm walking through is thick. The trees are tall. It's hot and humid, making the air seem even thicker and warmer. I'm dripping sweat, but I'm not giving up. I'm finding her. I can feel that she needs me.

"Baby, where are you? Come on. Talk to me. Tell me where you are. I can hear you."

"Cole," Dylan whispers again.

This time, it hits me right in the heart and makes me walk faster. I feel her pain. I feel her heart breaking. It's almost like she's been shattered, put back together, and now all of the shards of her are falling off piece by piece. If I don't get to her, there won't be anything left.

"Dylan! Where are you, my girl?"

"Here, my love. I'm right here."

Like she's really next to me, I feel her hand on my chest. I look down, but she's not with me. She's nowhere near me, and the forest I'm in slowly starts to fade away. I scream for her, but no sound comes out.

"Dylan," I croak out. It sounds loud in my mind, so I don't know why I can't hear myself say it.

"Shh… It's okay, baby. I'm right here."

I feel a hand over my heart, but it doesn't feel right. It doesn't feel like Dylan. The voice is too high-pitched. Annoying. It doesn't have the sexy and sultry Southern twang of my girl.

"Blood pressure is good, sir," another voice says. This one is soothing. Almost like a grandmother. I try to force my eyes open, but they feel heavy. Almost like they're glued shut.

"Stable across the board. Good. You're doing very well, Cole," another voice says. This one I know.

"Dr. Fr…" My throat feels dry. I swallow, but it's scratchy. I cough and feel instant pain in my chest and stomach. I groan.

"Easy, Cole." I feel hands on me. Larger than the woman's whose voice annoys the fuck out of me.

"Be still, baby."

Carmella. It has to be. But why the fuck would she be anywhere near me? One of the last things I remember is telling her we're not back together and to leave my house. I know I invited her over, but I did it to confront her. I remember having a couple of drinks. That's probably why I didn't just call her and bitch her out for ruining what I had going with Dylan.

"Dyl…an…" I cough again and groan as I lick my lips.

"Betty, I'd like you to get Dylan for me, please. Carmella, you can leave."

"Like hell. Can he have water?"

"Leave, Carmella," Dr. Freeman growls as I feel something against my lips. It's cold and wet. I greedily lick at it. "Easy, Cole. We can't have you aspirating."

I try to force my eyes open again as I listen to him and lick my now wet lips. Dr. Freeman keeps wetting my lips for a few moments until I feel like my throat is slightly satiated. Enough for me to gather what little strength I have to slowly open my eyes. It feels like there's sand in them.

I blink a few times. "Out," I say grittily. "Get out."

"What? Cole, no. You don't know what you're saying."

I turn my head only slightly, but meet her eyes with a furious glare. "Get… the… fuck… out," I growl.

"Baby, no. We just got back together. Don't you remember?"

I grit my teeth. "No."

"Well, we did. You fucked me that night."

I hear a gasp. I can't turn fast enough, but when I do, I see the petite body of my girl turning and fleeing the room. My heart breaks, but it's her words that infuriate me. "Get out!" I yell. It's not loud, but it's enough to make her jump in shock and my body to rebel on every level.

"Cole…"

"I know I didn't… fuck… you." I fight back the cough because I don't want to feel the pain that comes with it. Dr. Freeman gives me more water on a small sponge on a stick. When I finally get enough, I turn back to Carmella. It's obvious she has no idea what to say. "I may have fucked up and…" I close my eyes and clear my throat as gently as possible when it cracks. I slowly open them again because talking hurts as much as coughing. "And texted you. But I'd never fuck you and hurt the woman I love like that. I don't want… you… at all."

"Then why did you text me to come over, Cole? Huh? We -"

"The fuck we did." I don't remember a lot, but things are slowly coming back the longer I'm awake. Dr. Freeman gives me a little more water before taking the cup and standing up. I glare at Carmella. "I remember pushing you off me." I pause and wait for her to register my words. I'm still barely talking above a whisper, but it's enough to make her second guess her lie. "Are you… saying you… sexually assaulted me while I was… too fucking intoxicated to consent?" I ask, knowing damn well I have her. She may be a lot of things, but that's not something even she'd stoop to.

"Please fucking say yes," Dane says.

I turn slowly towards him and see Dylan standing in front of him. Her head is down. Her disheveled hair is falling over her beautiful face, and I want nothing more than to take her in my arms. She's not looking at me, but I don't need her to in order to feel the pain she does.

"I'd love to arrest you right here and now," Nick growls with a smirk as he steps out from behind Dane. "That would just make my fucking day. Come on. Confess."

"I didn't touch him, you fucking dick," Carmella spits.

"Oh, so that means he didn't fuck you, as you so eloquently put it?" Dane asks with a grin. I chuckle and let him handle it. All I care about is Dylan. She might be pissed at me, but just having her near goes a long way.

"I -"

"Get the fuck out, Carmella," Nick says.

"No! This isn't even between you or anyone else. Especially not that bitch. This is between us."

"She's not a bitch," I rumble. "Out."

"As entertaining as this is," Dr. Freeman interjects, "you're agitating my patient. Time to go."

"Excuse me? They're agitating him. Not me."

"Carmella, if you don't leave, I'll have these gentlemen escort you out. I promise they'll be more gentle with you than hospital security or Mr. Lucinio's guards. Now, leave this room immediately." Dr. Freeman has never messed around in all of the years I've known him. If he tells someone to do something, they'd best do it. He doesn't need the guards to fight his battles. The man is capable enough of doing it himself.

Carmella huffs but grabs her purse and storms towards Dylan. "This isn't over, you little bitch."

Before anyone can stop her, Dylan raises her head. I see the fire in her eyes, but I don't expect her to haul off and slap the shit out of Carmella. Carmella stumbles back, her hand automatically finding her cheek as she tries to process what just happened to her.

"Don't you ever talk to me like that again. You don't know who the fuck I am." Her voice is low and threatening. If I hadn't heard that tone several times over the past few weeks when she's been pissed at me, I'd be a little scared. "Now, leave before I personally make you regret being born."

"Damn," Nick says with a grin. "Didn't think I'd end up protecting the bitch from the quiet one today."

Dylan doesn't take her glare off Carmella, but Carmella recovers a little too quickly. "I want her arrested!"

"Who?" Dane asks as he pushes Dylan towards where Dr. Freeman is standing. "I don't see anyone. What are you talking about?"

"Oh my God, are you serious? You both saw her assault me!"

"I didn't see anything," Nick says with a shrug. "But I did hear the doctor tell you to get out."

"Fuck you both," Carmella growls.

"No thanks," Dane says as he grabs Carmella's arm.

Nick grabs the other. "That'll be a nope from me, too. I love my wife too much, but really, I wouldn't stick my dick in you if you were the last whore on this Earth." He shoves her a little roughly towards the door. I hear her yelling at them both all the way down the hall.

Dr. Freeman nods at Dylan before turning to me. "I'll let the others know you're awake and that you're okay but tired and need some time with your girl."

"Thanks, doc," I croak.

"I'll be back with ice chips." He looks down at Dylan. "Allow him only one spoonful every thirty minutes."

Dylan nods as he leaves. She looks down at the ground again, and I'm stunned for several moments before I'm able to speak. "You're so beautiful," I finally whisper.

She shakes her head. "I look awful," she whispers back, still looking at the ground.

"No, baby. You're beautiful."

She reaches up and rubs her eyes with a sniffle as she glances at me. "I've been so worried about you." Her voice cracks just before silent sobs wrack her body.

"Dylan. Don't cry, princess. Come here."

She steps towards me as the doctor comes back in. "Make sure you're just giving him the ice," Dr. Freeman says to Dylan as he hands her the cup with a spoon. She nods and wipes her eyes as he hurries back out.

Her lower lip quivers as I put my arm out and move over as far as I can and as carefully as possible to the side of the bed. She shakes her head. "You need your comfort to heal, Cole."

"I need you, Dylan. Come here."

As if the words are all she needs, she leans over me and puts the cup down on the table before quickly crawling into the bed with me. She's very careful not to move anything. She watches the IV in my other arm. She's cautious of the blood pressure cuff. When she finally lays down, she puts her head on my chest but keeps her arms wrapped around her middle.

114

"I was so scared," she whispers again. "I saw you once. You had so much stuff coming out of you. A machine was breathing for you. The IV. You had a bag attached to you."

I kiss her head and put my arm around her the best I can. "I'm sorry, baby. I'm sorry for all of this. It was stupid. Reckless. I didn't think I was near as intoxicated as I was. I still don't really know why I'm here, but I'm smart enough to figure some stuff out."

"They probably took the breathing tube and everything out when they woke you up." She takes a deep breath. "I don't know how much to tell you. I don't know if I'm allowed."

"I remember texting Carmella." I cough as gingerly as possible. The breathing tube thing she said was in me makes me understand why my throat and chest hurts. Dylan gives me some ice chips. It helps immensely. "She kissed me… after the press conference. I pushed her away and told her to get the fuck off me. When I got home and saw you leaving, I didn't know you saw that on TV."

"They didn't show you pushed her away."

"They wouldn't. She had a narrative to play. She played it very well later during the interview with her station." I'm still very scratchy talking, but I'm doing my best to give her the explanation she needs and deserves. "I remember going to Damon's to give you the sketchbook you forgot. I didn't look at it. I promise. I was going to explain everything and let you make your decision, but -"

"You saw me hugging Landon," she says quietly.

"Yeah," I growl a little more jealously than I mean to. "I guess it hit me harder than I care to admit."

"He's gay, you know. He has his eyes set on Ben."

I look down at her in shock. "What?"

"Mmhmm."

"Ben would be his direct supervisor. And I don't think he's gay."

"Mmhmm. It's why he's staying quiet about it. He hopes to stay on Ben's team as my personal guard, but he also recognizes that you hate it all and doesn't want to cause tension."

"First of all, while that does make me feel better, my behavior towards him was wrong. I'm not used to feeling the way I do about you. I'll admit that. I'm definitely protective over what's mine, but it still doesn't mean I should've acted like I have towards him. Second, none of that matters because you have every right to have friends. I wouldn't have done that with Dallas or Rosie. I never should've with him. I should've trusted you when you said he was a friend and left it alone."

Dylan is silent for so long, I'm sure she'll never forgive me for any of what I've done. Finally, though, she puts my fears of her never speaking to me again to rest. "You invited her over…?"

I let out a quiet breath and tangle my fingers in her hair. "More like demanded it. I wanted to confront her. I felt like in person was the best way. I was already drunk by then, but didn't really realize it. I know she showed up. I don't remember a lot of anything after that. I know I fell once. I know she was in my bed. I know I told her to leave and pushed her off. I passed out after that. It might not mean much, but I'm positive about that. I may have fucked up on many levels, but not on that one. I'd never sleep with her and hurt you like that."

She nods slowly. "Can I ask something?" she asks quietly as she picks invisible lint from my hospital gown.

"You can ask me anything you want." I fight back the yawn I feel coming. I've been fighting drifting off for a while. I refuse to do it without giving her what she needs from me.

"What are we?"

I smile softly into her hair as my eyes fall closed. I can't stop them, but I hug her tighter. "What do you want us to be?"

"Together," she whispers as her arm hesitantly wraps around me. "I just want to be yours."

"You are mine," I rumble as possessively as my tiring body lets me. "Forever…"

I drift off with my arm around her, and I'm just as peaceful as she always makes me.

Chapter Fifteen

☙ Dylan ☙

(Two Weeks Later)

I smile as I answer my phone. "Hello?"

"May I speak with Ms. Dylan Remington, please?" the dean of Kingston University, William Henderson asks.

"Speaking," I say cheerfully as I sit down at the kitchen table Cole has sitting next to a large window that looks over his backyard and pool.

"Ms. Remington, I'm following up on an email I received from the administration office and billing department as well as from the residence hall director from your dorm."

I raise an eyebrow. Cole sets a plate of fruit in the middle of the table and two plates with silverware. I put a plate on his side of the table and keep one for myself, then do the same with the silverware as I balance the phone between my ear and shoulder.

"Oh?" I ask, slightly confused and curious about what this could be about.

"I guess it's best to begin with on behalf of the school, we are sorry for the tragic loss of your father."

I glance up at the knock on the door as Cole pulls up a chair and positions it at the side of the small breakfast table. Cole walks to answer it. "Thank you, sir. That means a lot."

"Ms. Remington, on that note, we're aware that most students' parents are major proponents in the funding of their child or children's education."

I furrow my brows at my phone while Cole walks in quietly with a man I've only seen briefly and mostly in pictures. I swallow hard. Cain, or Ink, as he's known, walks in awkwardly. He's wearing jeans and a black leather jacket with several patches on it. I know from Blade they're called cuts. He has the same Viper's Venom patch that Blade does.

I clear my throat as Ink takes off his jacket, revealing a black t-shirt underneath, and hangs it off the back of the chair Cole gestures to him to sit in. "Oh, um…" I shake my head and focus back on the phone call as Cole sets down a third plate with silverware. "I understand you might believe there's a funding issue, but I actually have an account dedicated to my college education. We made sure the university financial office has that information. Payments should be taken directly from there each semester. There should be plenty to cover the expenses."

"I understand, Ms. Remington, but the office did try pulling money from the account for the room and board, and the transaction was declined with insufficient funds as the reason. That all being said, even if we get that resolved, which I'm sure we will quickly, I also have an email from the administration office regarding your enrollment as a whole. It says you've withdrawn and rescinded your acceptance. Also, the residence director informed me that you've informed him that you've canceled your meetings with him giving him the reason that you're no longer in need of the room and board."

My head is spinning. "Wait. I'm so sorry, sir, but that's a lot to take in. First, I never rescinded anything. I don't know where that came from, but I'm still planning and very excited to attend Kingston University. I just got my acceptance letter for the cheerleading squad. There's absolutely no intention of me withdrawing from anything."

Cole sets down the rest of breakfast, toast, eggs, and bacon, and looks at me as he sits down. His brows are furrowed just as mine are. Ink leans back in his chair and looks at me with the same expression Cole is.

"Okay, we'll need to get you here to sign a couple of things to make sure things are accurate with your enrollment. The other thing regarding the room and board. Our policy is that Freshman must stay on campus in the dorms."

I shake my head. "That's not something that's possible in my situation, sir. I need twenty-four hour protection from active threats to my life. According to previous conversations with both the university and the residence hall director himself, males aren't allowed in the female dorms. I asked for a transfer to a co-ed hall and was denied because they don't exist. My bodyguard is a male. If he's not able to be with me, as I need him to be, there is no other option for me but to choose housing that is more conducive to my safety and well-being. I was also denied a female bodyguard because the dorm doesn't allow guests who would be long term, which is what the university would consider my bodyguard. Because of this, my decision to remove myself from the dorms is one purely of safety."

"We have security that is available to you at all hours and all times. The dorms are secured. Your security detail is welcome to stay outside your dorm, but our policy is clear. As a Freshman, you need to be on campus. This goes for all Freshman, even residents of the city."

I rub my forehead. "Sir, I understand your position, but this is extenuating circumstances. My father was murdered in cold blood by a man still on the loose who is an active threat to me."

"Our campus is secure. Our security is very much aware of the situation. I can't budge on this because if I allow an exception for you, I need to allow it for everyone."

My mouth drops, and I rub my chest. "Sir, how many of these situations come up with students? Honestly? Is it every single year you have someone coming to you who is actively being threatened with death?"

"Well, no, but the policy is very clear, Ms. Remington."

Cole takes my phone and puts it on speaker before handing it back to me. "I understand the policy, but there has to be room for extenuating circumstances. If there's not, then people in my situation, who fear for their safety, would never go to your university. And I'm spending a lot of money there. Not only am I in extracurricular activities, but I'm also spending a lot of money on education, and that doesn't even count the donation that was made on my behalf just a month ago."

"While the university appreciates such a generous donation, it doesn't change the fact that this is a very serious ask. We have this policy in place for very specific reasons, the first being academic excellence and doing our part in starting our Freshman off on the right foot academically. That's something I won't budge on. Let's get back to the financial situation."

I take a breath and pull up my banking app. "Let me just get into my bank and figure out what's going on. There's just over a half-million in that account. There's no reason for anything to be denied." I log in as Cole and Ink watch me closely. When I see the numbers, my stomach drops. "Oh my God," I whisper.

"What? Let me see," Cole says, holding out his hand.

My entire body trembles as I do what he says and give him my phone. "Oh my God, Cole." I look at him with panicked, wide-eyes.

"Fuck," Cole whispers as he shows my phone to Ink.

"Who's that? Who's there? Ms. Remington?"

"Sir, my name is Cole Westwood. I'm a -"

"Sergeant with Chicago's finest. I know who you are."

Cole glances at the phone with a look of shock. "Listen, Dylan's account has been drained. There are no funds in there, which means this just became a case that will be handed over to a specialized taskforce led by Taylor Reddick."

"That doesn't solve -"

"You'll get paid. What's the deadline? I'll take care of it."

"Cole," I whisper.

"I can give you until Friday this week at 4pm."

"Okay. In the meantime, We'll get her paperwork taken care of, and someone will be in contact regarding your bullshit policy that supercedes the safety of your fucking students." Cole hangs up the phone and looks at Ink. "You thinking what I'm thinking?"

"Yep. The theory of her mother being with Ethan is absolutely true."

I put my head in my hands and groan. "This can't be happening. Cole, this was the one thing in my life that I had left. I can't let my dreams be torn from me like this."

"I'm not letting that happen, princess." He leans over and kisses my forehead. "But I need to talk to Josh and get Taylor on this right now.

So, I'm sorry to do this to you. I know you wanted me here while the two of you were introduced, but I think this needs to take precedence."

I nod. "No, you're right. You're right. This… needs to be fixed. I hope you can get that money back." I look up at him.

"It doesn't matter if I do or don't, Dylan. Your dreams are safe. I promise."

"Especially since I'll be funding your college," Ink says. Cole grins as he winks at me before leaving the kitchen and heading out of the house.

I look at Ink, bewildered. "Wh-what?"

He smiles and leans forward slowly. He starts putting food on his plate just as deliberately as he leaned forward. "This is going to sound a little crazy."

I don't know why, but that makes me laugh. "Are you kidding? Everything about my life for the past month has been pure insanity. Certifiably unbelievable. If I wrote a memoir about all of this, I'd surely be locked up. Nothing is more crazy than all of this."

Ink chuckles and starts putting food on my plate, though less portions than what he's given himself. "The day your mom left me and I saw that pregnancy test, I started putting away money for your college education or for whatever you wanted or needed it for once you became an adult. I never truly believed either of you were gone. I never stopped looking for either of you. The issue is there were a lot of blocks up, and I didn't have the resources to get through them. I had no leads. I had no way of knowing. When I first saw you when we got that call down there from Colton to Brystone Springs, I thought you looked a little like me, definitely like her, but I shoved it out of my mind. I didn't think there was anything I could do to prove it anyway." He takes a bite of his food and focuses on his plate.

I push my food around my plate. "Did you try?"

He smiles a little and nods. "Yeah. I did. I had your name run. I had your birth certificate pulled. I did everything in my power, but nothing ever panned out, just as it hadn't with her. Your age. That's all I really had to go on. I even had Lance help me out, but he didn't have enough to go on either. Whoever helped your mom gave her a very good new identity. All the bases were covered, which meant they all were with you, too."

"Lots of things make so much more sense now." I look down at my food, not really hungry. "My dad, well, I guess he's not really my dad." I look up at Ink with a sad smile.

He finishes his food in silence before pushing his plate aside and looking at me as he rests his forearms on the table. "Listen, honey. A dad isn't just someone biologically related to you, as I am. They're the ones who raise you. Teach you. They're the ones who are there for you guiding you throughout your life. I don't know a lot about Foster Remington. I know what Lance and Alec told me. I don't think he was the greatest man, but I do think, just by the way you seem to fondly say his name, that he did love you. And I'll be honest, that's all I could've hoped for. You with a loving family who cared about you and took care of you."

"I don't know how much they really cared for me," I say softly. "Apparently, I was sold to a madman before I was even born."

Ink chuckles darkly as he pulls his plate closer and piles more food on it. "Well, they failed. You did the right thing calling Dallas and Rosie and telling them what he said. And telling Colton and your cousin other things." He eyes my plate again, and I take that as my cue to put something in my mouth. I settle for the eggs.

Cole is an amazing cook. The eggs actually have taste to them. I'm not used to that. Usually what's sat in front of me is something that my mother cooked, and she's never been the greatest at it. Sometimes, my dad, well, my not dad, would take pity on me and take me out somewhere to eat. Usually it was times he couldn't stomach her food himself. I don't know how, but she always ate what she cooked. We used to joke about how there was no possible way she had taste buds.

"He, um… Foster? He… had some strange conversations the past couple of years. One of them was something about my birthday. How it wasn't the agreement or the right time. I didn't know what he was talking about then, but I guess now I feel like he was talking to Ethan. I was sixteen." I put my fork down, unable to eat the food, even though it's tasty.

Ink pats my arm. "It's okay. You don't need to force yourself. Want to try a fruit shake? I make a pretty mean one."

I smile genuinely as I nod. "That would actually be amazing. I don't usually have a problem like this."

122

"Well, I'm also pretty sure you don't usually have this kind of a fucked up day either." He stands and clears my plate out of the way, leaving his. He takes the fruit with him.

"Or fucked up month," I mumble.

"You've gone through a lot, Dylan. More shit than most. It sounds to me like Foster did love you, though. I think Ethan was probably trying to make him hand you over at sixteen. What makes little sense to me is all of the rest. When did Mackenzie meet Ethan? How the fuck did she run from a biker only to end up with one? Why did she take off in the first place? And why have you if she knew I'd be after her and looking for her?" He shakes his head and starts the blender. A few moments later, he stops it and pours my shake in a glass. He brings it to me and sets it down. "Anyway, there are a lot of questions I'm sure we both need answers to."

"You're seriously not joking." I take a drink of the shake as Ink, or dad, I guess, eats.

When he's finished, he stands and starts cleaning up. "That's really not a conversation for today. Today was meant to be a day for us to get some one-on-one time. Get to know each other."

"I'm honestly pretty excited. I just really want to start a new chapter. I'm worried about school, though."

"Well, I can assure you that Josh will deal with the room and board thing. You don't need to worry. It'll be dealt with by the end of the day. And you don't need to worry about funding it. There's more than enough in the account I set up for you."

I'm quiet for a few minutes while he does the dishes. After finishing my shake, I take a deep breath as I stand to bring him the cup. "It's just that Kingston University is a top ten school. It's really elite and expensive." I put the cup in the sink. "It's not that I don't think you -"

"Have enough?" He grins cockily down at me, but my heart physically hurts.

"Well, that you have enough to cover. It's going to be like two-hundred thousand with the books and extracurricular activities. And if we do end up going to state or nationals or something, I have to pay for that because the university can't cover all of that. I guess I don't know how much they do or if I'll even make the cuts, but I need that safety net, you know?"

He finishes the last of the dishes and turns to me as he dries his hands. I lean against the counter on the other side of him. "You said you had just about a half-million."

I nod, sadly. "A little more. It's not even about the loss of it. I mean, it's scary because that would've lasted me a long time, but I'm so mad she took it. I don't even know how she had access."

"She's got a lot of resources, sweetheart. She has people who can change her identity. You said it yourself to Cole. She looks like she could be your sister. That means with a little makeup, she probably could look just as young as you. Now, imagine her going in there with an ID and your name. No one would bat an eye, right?"

I nod. "I really hate that you're right."

"Listen, Dylan. I promise you don't have to worry. Firstly, Viper's Venom is a huge organization, and I get paid well. Secondly, I didn't have a lot of shit to spend my money on as I got older. I spent some time with drugs and alcohol. I have a nice rap sheet for fucking up while I was drunk or high. But when it came down to it, the one thing that kept me from completely going over the edge was the idea I had in my mind that you and Mackenzie were okay. The older I got, the more I believed that she left. I had my slip ups, but in the end, I felt like she left. And if she left willingly, the chances she had you were high. So, I kept putting money away for you. I hoped that when you came of age, it would make it easier to find you, or that you'd seek me out. Our meeting isn't the way I imagined at all. It took some time to process it, but you're here now. I'm here. We move on. When we catch them, we'll get our answers, but in the meantime, life is just as it was. Only, a couple key players are now linked, which makes us unstoppable. That money I put away is over a half-mill. It's a lot closer to a million."

I look up at him with furrowed brows. "What?"

He crosses his arms over his chest. "Yeah. I thought college. A nice down payment on a house. Or hell, even some traveling if that's what you wanted. And if I never found you before my death, I was going to befriend a little orphan girl who reminded me of you. I was going to have someone I was close to adopt her. And then I was going to give all of the money to her. That was the plan."

"What about kids of your own?" I ask.

"Mackenzie was the love of my life. I really hadn't intended on sharing my life with anyone else." He looks down but recovers so quickly, that I wonder if I imagined the longing look I saw. Does he have someone in his life that he's in love with who he simply won't tell out of fear of losing her? "Anyway, college is paid for. You're set. Don't worry about college. What do teenagers like to do? Should we go to the zoo?" He grins wickedly. "No, no, no! That's not right. It's the mall, right?"

I laugh. "Actually, I love the sound of the zoo, but I do need to pick up a few things. I really don't have a lot of clothing, and Josh basically banned me from going back to Texas to grab anything out of the house I lived in. Colt is going to grab things off a list I gave him. Things that are just important or sentimental to me, but there's a lot of stuff I need that I don't have."

"Then the mall it is."

"I still have to call the university and get this mess straightened out."

"Something tells me Cole has that under control. So, the mall it is. Call your bodyguard, kid. We're heading out."

I can't help but giggle as I follow him as I text Landon. Cole has done an amazing job of making me happy, but I've been worried. My mood right now is lighter than it has been in days. For the first time in weeks, I feel my guard coming down more and more. Hope fills me. Maybe everything will turn out alright after all…

Chapter Sixteen

🍎 Cole 🍎

I finish setting up my den for my date night with Dylan. She's been texting me throughout the day with Ink and saying what a great time she's been having. They've spent all day at the mall. They had lunch together. Dylan mentioned her feet are killing her, so I've got pizzas in the oven, an all meat, also a veggie style, and I'm turning the den into something she'll love.

Like the penthouse, I have a sectional couch. With a couple of movements, the couch becomes a large bed. I spread a fitted sheet over it, followed by a flat one. I grab the large fleece blanket she loves, and then put a comforter on top of it. I position the pillows along the cushions of the couch, then walk to the kitchen to grab the pizzas.

Once I have everything cut and set up in the den, I hear her come in. Her melodic laughter rings through my house, and I smile because I love the sound. I meet her in the living room. Ink is behind her carrying her bags.

"That looks like a lot of stuff," I say with a grin as I lean down and kiss her.

"So much, but I got everything I needed. I only had a couple pairs of jeans and a couple shirts. I was washing things like every other day."

"I know, baby. Why don't you head upstairs and change into something comfy? Then, come meet me in the den."

"Yes, Sergeant." She gives me a sexy grin before skipping up the stairs.

I groan as Ink comes back down the stairs after bringing her stuff to the bedroom. He's about the same size as me, just a little more muscular. He grins and shakes his head at my groan. "You've got your hands full will her."

"I know." I laugh.

"She couldn't stop talking about you, man. She's head over heels."

My heart leaps, and I smile. "The feeling is mutual."

"As her father, it's my obligation to say be nice to my girl, or I'll bury you. I have a twelve-gauge and shovel just waiting for the occasion, and they'll never find you." He tries to look serious, but I can see the happiness dancing in his eyes.

"Noted. How did it go?"

"Good. We talked a lot. She had a pretty good life growing up. Her cousins, even though they aren't, are still her best friends. She said they've been through a lot together, and she's glad they still accept her."

"That was something very important to her. She's gained a lot here and with finding out about you and the truth, but they're very important to her."

"That and school."

"Yeah, about that. Josh got them to bend the rules for her. She doesn't have to stay in the dorm. I don't even think it was intimidation this time. I think it was the threat of his attorneys. They know he has an endless amount of money to fight them, and they wouldn't win anyway. It really is for her safety. They can't guarantee her or us that she'll be okay."

"I think they know they're in the wrong on that one. What about the rest of the stuff?"

"The tuition and stuff?"

"Yeah. I've been putting money away. There's close to nine-hundred thousand in there. She's set for a while."

"Yeah, Alec mentioned it. Josh wants you to keep it under your name. Lance is doing something tech related with it to safeguard it. I couldn't begin to even tell you. Some wall and barrier and shield. All I can think of is he's building the goddamn Roman Empire around it."

Ink laughs. "Yeah, Alec texted me for the account information. He said something about Lance protecting it and then Josh dealing with the school and financial stuff."

"He got the new account number to them. Dylan has an appointment tomorrow to sign some stuff. You'll have to be with her since the account is under your name. Lance explicitly said like a hundred times to leave it that way for now."

"I figured. If her college account can be drained like that, it's best to not have anything in her name."

We both look up the stairs before I sigh. "This needs to be over in one week. School is starting in two weeks, but practice for cheerleading starts next week. I do not want to complicate things and isolate her."

"I know." He claps my shoulder and gives me a one armed hug that I return.

Once he leaves, I start shutting off the lights. My plan is to stay in the den tonight. "Coming, baby?" I call up the stairs. I don't want to shut off the stair light and leave her in the dark.

"Coming!" She hurries down the stairs wearing one of my t-shirts.

My dick is at immediate attention. "Fuck, sexy girl. What are you trying to do to me?"

"Seduce you?" She stops on the last stair and kisses me before darting to the den.

I slap her ass and laugh as I shut out the light and follow her. When I get to the den, she's already happily under the covers waiting for me. I close the door and crawl in next to her. I'm only wearing a pair of gym shorts, and I'm happy that was my decision because she looks like she wants me more than the food.

That is until she catches the scent of the food. "Pizza. Oh my gosh, yes."

I grin. "And here I thought it was me you were looking at so hungrily."

"Well, it was. And then the food hit my senses, and I realized I'm starving."

I laugh. "By all means, dig in." I find the new movie she wanted to watch and grin when she sees what it is.

"Oh! *Portrait*? I've been dying to see this one."

"You were talking about it the other day. I saw it on Netflix. I thought we could do this one, and then *Shutter Island* since we didn't get to finish it that first movie night we had. I love that movie. I've watched that movie like five times, and I still catch something new every single time that makes me just wonder what the fuck I just watched."

She giggles, then looks at me with wide eyes. "Do we still have ice cream?"

I wink. "I picked some up earlier."

"If you say cake batter, this will be the best day of my life."

I give her a sexy grin. "If cake batter ice cream is the best day of your life, I don't have much work to do to wow you."

She laughs. Fuck me, I love her laugh. "But I love when you go all romantic."

I put a hand to my chest in feigned shock. "What are you talking about? Me? No. I don't do all that romance shit. This is all just so you'll ride me later."

She pushes me with another giggle that makes my heart skip. "I'd believe you, but I know the you underneath the asshole exterior."

"Well, fuck me. I need to refortify them walls," I drawl in my best Southern accent.

"If you talked like that in Texas, you'd be shot on the spot."

"Excuse me, princess. Not all of us can be perfect with a sexy Southern accent like you." I roll my eyes teasingly and go back to my pizza.

"You think my accent is sexy?" She looks up at me curiously, her pizza paused halfway to her mouth.

"I think all of you is sexy. Your voice is really just one more thing to love."

She blushes and takes a bite of her pizza. She doesn't say anything, but she does press closer to me. I kiss her head. When we finish eating, I clean up while she gets more and more engrossed in the movie. I keep my eyes on the screen as I move our plates and empty drinks to the table at the side of the couch. I crawl back into the bed and wrap an arm around her so I can pull her close and rub her feet.

Deep into the second movie, though, I find myself with my tongue deep in Dylan's pussy and her writhing underneath me. I grip her hips a little harder and push her down more into the bed couch underneath her pretty ass.

"Cole!" Her fingers tangle in my hair. She tugs me closer to her sexy wetness, and I thrust my tongue in as deeply as I can. I growl low knowing full well the vibration from my voice reverberates through her. "Oh… yes… yes!" she moans. She tries to arch into me, but I have her right where I want her. I keep her pressed down.

"Patience," I rumble, making her thighs tremble. I nip her pussy and pull away.

"No, no, no, no! Cole!" she pants. "That's like the hundredth time."

I laugh as I slowly tug my sweats and boxer briefs off. "Fifth. It was the fifth. And while I love the taste of you all over my tongue," I say as I crawl over and position my dick right at her entrance. "I have no intention of letting you come on my tongue tonight." I slam into her.

She screams out and grips my shoulders. Her hips arch into mine with a force that sinks me deeper inside her. "Fuck, Cole!"

Her pussy is already spasming for me, so I quickly grip her hips and flip us both over so she's on top of me. "I've been thinking of you riding me all day." I slap her ass, making her jerk into me with a gasp. "So, do it."

Shyly, because that's how it always starts, she braces herself by placing her hands on my abs. She looks down at our connection and starts moving up and down. It's slow and very deliberate, but her sexy moans and gasps are just as much of a turn on to me as her pussy taking my dick is.

I keep my grip on her hips and guide her. I've learned very quickly that while she's very witty and keeps up with me on every level, including my dark humor and sarcasm, she's also very submissive, especially in the bedroom. She needs guidance. She doesn't function without it. Guidance makes her feel sure of herself. When she's sure of herself and her actions, she lets loose. When she lets loose, it ends up being the best sex I've ever had, each time topping the one before.

I move her back and forth as she lifts herself off me and slides back down over my shaft again and again. Her eyes stay on my cock entering her. She still can't get over my length, despite how many times I'm inside her. I'm just over nine inches and thick. She's afraid she'll stretch out, and she won't feel as tight to me, which she knows I love, but there's no way I see that happening.

She lets her head fall back. Just as I love her tightness, she loves the way I fill her. The moment I start thrusting inside of her is when she loses control. My favorite thing is when she loses all sense, and I get to bring her back.

She leans back and grips my thighs. "Holy fuck," I growl as I thrust. Just the motion tightens her pussy around me, but because she loves making me as hard as she possibly can, she clenches repeatedly around my dick, making my eyes roll back at how fucking good she feels. "Fuck, baby."

"I'm so close." She meets my thrusts until we're both pounding ourselves against each other. She gets wetter and wetter as I get thicker and thicker. Her pussy pulses with each uncontrollable thrust.

Keeping one hand firmly on her ass, I move the other to her perfectly smooth pussy. "Come," I command. I need to feel her. I press my thumb against her clit and start rubbing in a circular motion to the rhythm of my thrusts.

Her nails rake down my abs, and I moan. "Cole!" she screams as her entire body quivers for me. I pound into her during the entirety of her orgasm but hold her still so she can feel every ridge and thrust I give her through every second of her own pleasure.

When I feel her pussy start to tighten even more, signaling a second orgasm is on the way, I stop thrusting and rubbing her clit. "Fuck, princess," I groan as my own release hits. My hips jerk against hers as my dick thickens. I come deep inside her at the same time her second orgasm sweeps over her. I watch her eyes roll back. She takes everything I give as I shout, "Dylan!"

She collapses on my chest and rolls off me onto her back, panting. "Oh my God," she whispers. "I still can't believe how good that feels."

I grin. "It all depends on your partner. Some aren't that good."

"Thank you for being that good." She giggles. I laugh as she curls into my side like it's instinct. "We might have to restart the movie."

I glance at the screen and chuckle. "Yeah, it's almost to the end."

"I still don't understand what happens in this movie. It's so twisted."

"It's one of my favorites." I restart the movie from the beginning.

"Then, help me make sense of it."

I grin. "Well, basically there's this island called Shutter Island. It holds an insane asylum for the criminally insane. These two US Marshals, Teddy and Chuck, go there because someone very dangerous mysteriously escapes from a locked room. They go to find her, but while on the island, Teddy, played by Leonardo DiCaprio, starts experiencing issues and flashbacks to his time in the war. From there, things start getting complicated."

"Yeah, you're telling me."

I run my fingers through her hair. "I'll explain as we go, but basically what happens is Teddy reveals to his partner, Mark Ruffalo's character, that he really took the case to find the arsonist, Andrew Laeddis, who murdered his wife. He eventually breaks into an off-limits wing of the hospital, and meets a man who appears to know him. He tells him not to trust anyone, especially his partner, Chuck. He tells him some people get taken to the lighthouse to get lobotomized."

"Eew. That part I did understand. It's really the other crazy stuff. I don't know who Teddy ends up actually being, and how we even get there."

"Well, Teddy is actually Andrew Laeddis. He's a US Marshal who killed his manic depressive wife after she killed their kids. He had his own psychotic break. He ends up remembering everything. His partner is really a doctor. The lead doctor on the island warns him that if he relapses into a state like this again where they have to do this whole elaborate game with him, he'll lobotomize him because he's violent with staff and guards. On the way back to the hospital, he tells Chuck, who is supposedly a doctor named Dr. Sheehan, that they need to get off the island. He slips and calls him Chuck again, appearing delusional once more. So, Sheehan signals to the lead doctor that it's happened again. Orderlies come to take him for the lobotomy, but before he leaves with them, he turns to Sheehan and asks him if it's better to live as a monster or die a good man. Sheehan slips and calls him Teddy instead of Andrew as he's walked to the lighthouse."

"Wait. So, he's really a good guy?"

"Not exactly. He really is Andrew. The hospital staff went along with his delusion to guide him back to reality and help him to confront his past. At the end, Andrew knows what he did, but believes what he did was justified. He believes he's a good man who did some kind of vigilante justice. He went to get the lobotomy to end his own suffering."

"But lobotomies didn't kill everyone, did they? I mean there was no guarantee that he would die."

"True, but his point was even if it worked, he'd never be the same man. Also, they eluded through the movie that lobotomies were done to control them, so they were done differently and often killed people instead. There were lots of deaths, too, which is how the entire delusion started. The woman he was looking for disappeared. In his mind, she was dangerous and escaped. He and his partner had to find her. The lucid part of him believed people were dying because of the lobotomies. When they brought him back to reality, he realized that if he had one done, his chances of survival would be low. If he survived it, he'd live the rest of his days trapped in his own mind and body. A good man, or a monster."

"Oh…, wow. I thought I was super good at following movies like that, but none of any of that I really understood. The ending just completely baffled me, but it all makes perfect sense now. Basically, he killed his wife because she killed his kids, and it just broke him."

"Exactly. So, everything that happens after that is in his own mind."

"I can't really blame him for taking justice into his own hands and breaking like that. That's so horrible."

I smile and hug her closer. "I think the twists and turns; the complete mindfuck is why I like it so much."

"Me too," she murmurs as she wraps her naked body around me.

I chuckle because I know she's not going to last the entire movie. I pull the blankets up over us both and adjust the pillows. Once I'm settled, her body molds itself to me. A lot of men have issues sleeping this close to a woman they claim to love, and I've never understood it. I'm like that with women I don't care about. I want my space.

With Dylan, it hasn't been like that. It wasn't like that from the moment I met her. I wanted her near me all the time, but I also knew myself well. Best to be an asshole so I didn't ruin her. What I didn't expect was for her to stand up to me and give it back to me just as well. Her strength and drive are admirable.

I don't know if I'm ready to tell her, but I'm in love. I don't know when it happened. It's not something I've ever truly felt before, not on this level, but it's something I refuse to ever let go. Dylan is mine to keep; to love; to protect, defend, cherish, and honor.

Dylan is mine.

Chapter Seventeen

❦ Dylan ❦

(One Week Later)

"Go Dragons!" I cheer hitting a perfect right diagonal just after a back handspring.

"Yes! Dylan, that was perfect!" Steph yells from the sidelines. She's the head cheerleader and is bringing us through our first full routine as a team. We're to perform it at half-time at the first football home game in just over three weeks from today. I'm so incredibly excited for it. "Maryann! That tumble looked incredible! Jenna, I think we need to work on the splits a little more. It looks like you're a little untrusting of yourself, but once you commit, you're all about it!"

Jenna nods. "Yes, ma'am. I'm a little afraid to land them."

"Don't be! You're flexible and land them perfectly. Don't think about anything more than the next move. Thinking of everything as a whole and who's watching makes everyone nervous. If you just think of the next move, you'll be fine. At the end just focus on your last move, your finish, which is just waving your pom poms or spirit fingers or smiling."

"Thank you, Steph," Jenna says with a big smile. "That helps so much."

Steph smiles encouragingly. "Okay, practice is done for the day. Get yourselves something to drink before you go. Hydration is so important!" Everyone starts jogging to the sidelines, but Steph comes towards me. "Dylan, can you hang back just a minute?" She looks around nervously.

"Oh, yeah. Of course. What's up? Is it the security here?"

Her eyes widen slightly as her co-captain walks towards us. Austin. Steph shakes her head. "No, it's nothing like that. We understand the situation and appreciate you being upfront with us from the get-go."

"Our concern," Austin begins, "is the guy who's been in the parking lot since we started practice."

I furrow my brows and look around the stadium. "You can't see the parking lot from here."

"We know. But we had someone come up to us during that last routine and mention it. It was one of the football players. They're about to take the field for practice." Austin looks over his shoulder. "You have two guys here, but this guy looked pretty big."

"Like, really big," Steph says.

I nibble my lip. "I have Landon and Ben. They're both armed." I hug myself, suddenly very uncomfortable and not having Cole near me. The next best thing for me would be Dane, but he's working with Cole. "Maybe I should call Josh," I whisper. "He's the next best thing after Cole and his best friend, Dane."

"Well, we have an idea," Steph begins, looking up at Austin. It's always been pretty obvious they're a couple, but it's never been more obvious than now. The two are so adorable together.

Austin gives her a soft smile before they both look back at me. "We thought I could head back to the locker room and grab the football team. Even if he's armed, he can't take on all of us. Both teams combined, you know?"

I let out a breath. "I don't know. Maybe? I really just want to get out of here. We can call Josh from the car. I'll tell Landon and Ben." I hurry to them as Austin nods and jogs to the locker room. Steph goes to gather the cheerleaders.

As soon as Landon sees me, the smile drops from his face. "What's wrong? I was just about to send Ben out to scope things out so we can get out of here."

I shake my head. "Don't. One of the football players told Austin and Steph some big guy was outside."

Ben immediately reaches for his gun as Landon grabs his phone. "Where?" Ben asks.

I put a hand on his arm. "I think… we're going to show a united front. Whoever that is can make a move before we can. If it's Ethan, I think he's just showing that he can get to me. He may try to make a move against the two of you, but he won't against all of them." I point towards the ramp where all of the football players are coming out of. "Or them." I nod towards the cheerleading team.

Landon shakes his head. "No. No, no, no. We're calling for backup. We don't know how many people are out there with him. I'm sure he has a gun."

"Then you and Ben lead us out. He needs to be shown he can't intimidate me, which is what he's trying to do. I'm not some scared little girl, and I have people on my team without the mafia. That's what he needs to see."

"Dylan, absolutely not. It's n-"

Ben puts a hand on Landon's shoulder. His gun is still in his other hand, and he doesn't take his eyes off me, though Landon's head snaps to his face. "Wait. She's right. If he's anything like what his dad is or his brother is, he'd have shown up with force. They'd be visible. He wouldn't even attempt to hide them. He knows we scope out the place and have eyes all over, even if he doesn't see them. He wouldn't dare show with force, but he would show up alone. Less conspicuous. He'd scope the place to see how many people we have here. He'd see that it's just us visible."

"So… you're saying… what?" Landon asks.

Ben looks at him. "I'm saying she's right. If it's Ethan out there, which would surprise me, but if it is him and not just one of his disposable henchmen, he'd be alone. He's cocky enough to think he can overpower us when he sees it's just us. He would think he'd have enough time to take us out before grabbing her. In and out, no matter how many people are hiding."

Landon sighs and rubs his head. "Do not get me fucking killed. By him or Josh."

Ben grins. "Trust me."

The quarterback, also one of the football team's captains, puts his arm around my shoulder and hugs me. "What are we waiting for? We don't let anyone fuck with one of our own," Kelce says. He has to be around six-five or something. He's all muscle. It's really no wonder he's so unstoppable. The rest of the team is filled with big guys.

Landon runs a hand down his face. "This is a terrible idea." He shakes his head as he takes out his own gun and readies it.

"It's a fantastic idea. He'll bolt the second he sees anyone on our side bolting into the parking lot to catch him. My guess is he's on a bike." Ben drops his hand from Landon's shoulder as he turns.

"What difference does that make? We can surround him," Landon argues as we all follow Ben.

"A big one. There's only one entrance and exit for this lot. But it's bordered by woods that lead to the lakeshore. He can easily escape that way. We couldn't follow in SUVs."

"Then we call Alec." Landon reaches for Ben's arm. "Ben, wait." Ben turns, and Landon lets his hand fall. "Seriously, I don't want anyone in harm's way."

"Trust your partner," Ben says. "I've been doing this a long time."

Landon sighs and nods. "Okay." He lets out a breath and turns towards me and the football team. He takes my shoulders and puts me between the two biggest guys on the team. Kelce and James, a tight end, separate enough for me to stand between them.

Cheerleaders fade in with football players as we follow Ben and Landon. Even though the two of them are ahead of me, I can see Ethan as clear as day. He's leaning against his motorcycle with his arms folded across his chest. He's wearing a dark t-shirt with a vest that has his patches on. He definitely resembles Josh and Alex. He's as tall and large as they are. Just as intimidating. I find myself inadvertently stepping a little further behind the two football stars.

"Calm down. I come in good faith," Ethan says. "At the risk of my brother turning up at any fucking moment." He stands to his full height. "And my boss coming after me." He starts to reach in his back pocket. I whimper and brace myself for a shoot out.

"Hey! Hands where we can see them!" Landon commands. He and Ben have both their guns instantly trained on Ethan.

Ethan freezes and shows his hands slowly. "I have an envelope in my back pocket."

"I don't trust you for a fucking second," Ben barks. "Turn around."

Ethan does as Ben commands. He turns around with both hands in the air, revealing a yellow manilla envelope that looks like it's folded to fit in his pocket. "See? Envelope."

"Don't fucking move, Ethan," Ben growls as he moves forward.

"I know you have a hard on for bringing me to your boss, but it's a fucking mistake. You need to let me work. I'm close to leading Josh right to him, but you have to trust me."

"I have absolutely no reason to trust you. You've been enough hassle. I'm taking you in."

Ethan remains as still as possible. "I get it. I do. I know you have no reason to trust me, but keep this in mind. I got Cole to get Dylan out of the penthouse before my boss got there. He was planning a complete takedown. Your guards would've had no warning at all. I'm here right now running the risk of you doing exactly what you're doing. You need to let me go."

"Not a chance," Ben says. He glances at Landon, who gives him a head nod. We're close enough to Ethan that if Ben needs help, Landon will be right there. And so will everyone else.

"Just take the envelope and back away from me. I won't move. I'll stay right here. When you see what's in there, you'll understand."

"I'd feel a lot better with you in cuffs."

"Fine. But you need to make this quick. I'm risking both my life and a lot of other people's by being here."

I stand still, confused beyond belief, as Ethan allows Ben to cuff him. Ben takes the envelope and opens it. Ethan stays facing away from him. "What the hell is happening?" I murmur. "Should I call Josh?"

"Jesus Christ," Ben says. "No. No. Don't call Josh." He puts his gun in its holster and envelope in his back pocket before quickly uncuffing Ethan. "I already texted him 911. He's on his way."

"What?" I shake my head, even more confused.

"Go, Ethan. Get the fuck out of here. Through the woods. Hide until we're gone." Ben walks back to us as Ethan jumps on his bike. He glances at me and winks before firing up his bike and speeding away towards the woods. Ben hands me the envelope. "The money that was taken from you is in there. I'm really fucking sorry, Dylan, but this is going to crush you. We need to get you home. Now." He looks up at my team. "Thank you, all of you for your bravery. That takes a lot of guts."

"Like I said. We protect our own." Kelce holds out his hand and shakes Ben's before signaling everyone back to the field.

Steph hands me my bag. "Don't forget. Water. Hydrate."

On impulse, I hug her. "Thank you. So much."

"You're welcome, sweetie. I hope this all ends soon."

"Me too." As she walks back to the field with Austin, I take my place between Ben and Landon. "Now what?"

"Now, we wait for Josh, and we hope he doesn't shoot me on the spot," Ben says calmly. My mouth drops.

Landon bends over at the waist and dry heaves. "Oh fuck. I hate you. I fucking hate you."

Ben pats him on the back. "Don't worry. You'll be safe."

"Motherfucker. I'm kicking your ass. I fucking swear it."

"Is he really going to kill you?" I almost whisper, trying to figure out any way possible to keep that from happening.

"Guess we're about to find out," Ben says just as a swarm of black SUVs fly into the lot at a high rate of speed. They form a circle as everyone jumps out with weapons drawn.

Josh steps out of the back of an SUV that screeches to a stop right in front of us. "Where is he, Ben? Are my eyes deceiving me? Because I don't fucking see him."

I take this moment to grow my own set of balls and step in front of both Landon and Ben. I stand toe to toe with Josh. "Something happened. They made a call that will be the best for all of us. Ethan isn't the bad guy."

Landon finally stands up and groans as he puts his gun away. "It's been nice knowing you."

Josh raises an eyebrow, but his piercing blue eyes still cut through my soul. "Start talking."

"He showed up and gave us an envelope. The envelope has all of the money that was taken from me. He also said something about getting Cole to get me out of the penthouse before his boss showed up."

"He gave us evidence and picture proof on who his boss is."

Josh looks at Ben and holds out his hand. Ben hands him what looks like a letter. Josh opens it. There are several pictures. He scans the letter and the pictures. With each second that passes, it looks like he's getting more and more upset.

When he finally finishes, he shakes his head. "This is un-fucking-believable."

"That's what I said," Ben says. "It's why I made the decision I did."

"It was the right one," Josh agrees as he looks at me.

"I have no idea what's happening, and neither does Landon," I tell him honestly.

Josh nods. "Landon and Dylan with me. Ben, you can take my driver and follow us." He pauses and glances around at his men. "Everyone else, move out. We're done here."

It's then I realize that Josh has an earpiece in his ear. I've always thought he was smart and well-prepared. This small thing is just one more that seals that thought to me. I follow Josh to the SUV. Landon gets in the driver's seat. Josh gets in the passenger seat. I get in the back.

Once we're all in and on the road home, I say, "So? What's going on?"

"Sweetheart, I'm gonna be honest. I don't want you knowing what I know until we're home and you have Dallas, Rosie, and Cole with you. I will tell you this, though. Everything just changed. Everything. And I'm really not sure how to proceed. I need a plan. I need to get together with my team. I'm going to team up with Crane Mafia and Viper's Venom on this one. And when it's all over, the entire dynamic of this family is likely going to change irrevocably."

"Yeah, that makes me feel a whole better, Josh." I rub my chest.

Josh turns around and holds out his hand for mine. I glare at it but finally place mine in his. "We have a much larger enemy to take down than I thought. I need all the help I can get because I don't know how far he's nestled himself into the cockles of this country or any others. This needs to be handled delicately, tactfully, and with every single contact in all world governments that we have. Because what I have in my hand, honey, is a nuclear bomb in danger of exploding. And if it does, nothing is ever going to be the same. You have to trust me. You need the support. I will tell you everything you want to know and need to, but you have to have your support system around you."

I take a deep breath and nod. I'm not sure it makes me feel better, but I understand his reasoning and position. The issue is that I think I already know who the larger enemy is.

Josh squeezes my hand before letting it go. At a red light when Landon stops, Josh shows him something that makes him gasp.

"Jesus Christ," Landon says.

I close my eyes. My suspicions are all but confirmed. Country. World governments. There's only one man I know other than Josh Lucinio and Ryan Crane who have that kind of power.

My father…

Chapter Eighteen

❦ Cole ❦

I lean back in my chair and stare at the screen in front of me as I lock my fingers behind my head and narrow my eyes. My hope is that if I glare it into submission, the information I seek will appear. The problem is that I'm not a financial crimes type of man. This is Taylor's team's wheelhouse, but I really wanted something to pop out at me while they're working on it.

It's just that something is bothering me about Dylan's money. Something I can't let go of. I've been waiting for security footage, but Colton is having problems getting it. As luck would have it, so is Lance. It's almost like the footage was wiped.

I glance up as someone knocks on the door of the office I'm in. It's not in use right now, so I use it for a retreat when I need to get the fuck out of the bullpen and think. Matt slips in, closing the door behind him. He sits in a chair across from me.

"How's it going?"

"I don't know." I lean forward. "I'm struggling with some shit. It doesn't add up."

"The connection of Dylan's account to all of this?"

"Yeah, it doesn't make sense. From what I can tell, Foster Remington is the only one who had access to that account. I asked Dylan if she had debit cards or anything that were directly linked to that account. She thought she did. She gave it to me. Reed from Taylor's team did a track on it. It leads to her own personal account. Not that one. And her personal account isn't connected to the college one at all. There's no way for it to be drawn from by her. The account number she had and what the school had are two completely separate accounts. She had no idea. She thought the number she was given, which was written on the back of one of her dad's business cards, was the college account. The login she had for it was different from the one she uses for her own banking. She was told that money was hers to pay for school with. When she became a Sophomore, she was supposed to be able to use it for an apartment."

"Have you tracked that account number? The one she had?"

"Reed did. Taylor double checked, and then had both Robby and Lance triple check. Then for kicks, I did. The account doesn't exist."

"So, she was given a fake number. The college was given the real number."

I nod. "Yep. Doesn't make sense, but the other thing throwing me is that she doesn't have access. Her mother doesn't have access, so my theory of her mother going in dressed like her with her ID doesn't make sense."

"How did the money get withdrawn then? Foster's dead."

"Right again. And it was withdrawn after his body was found. A week after, to be exact. Maybe two. I don't fucking know anymore." I reach up and rub my temples. "Everything I'm thinking can't possibly be right."

"Run it by me. What are you thinking?"

I chuckle. "That Foster Remington isn't dead. Colton never got a positive ID on the body. It was too mangled. DNA was sent for testing. It hasn't come back yet."

"Typical. Even putting priority on it doesn't help."

"I've never run into the issue. I've worked at LAPD and here. We have our own lab, so I could be on them until I got it. He had to send his off."

"Yeah, we did in Gainesville, too. What about security footage from the bank?"

"It's been requested. Colton hasn't received it. He went in with a warrant for it. They didn't have it. He took the entire system. Lance flew out to help him, but all he has right now is that it's been erased."

"Backup files?"

"He knows they're there, but they're buried. He's working on it. Even sent for Robby, but both of them are seemingly against a hacker that knows what they're doing." I drop my hands back to the desk. "I feel like I'm just running headfirst into brick wall after brick wall."

"Well, put it away. Carmella is here to see you."

"Nope. Tell her to fuck off."

Matt chuckles as he stands. "You know I'd have no issue with that, but something is nagging at me. She looks scared."

"Probably because she knows she fucked up."

"Nah. It's something else. I made her wait because I want to see if anything changes with that expression before I send her in here." He walks out of the office.

I sigh. "Motherfucker." I snap the folder I'm looking at closed and put it away. I don't trust her at all, and the file I'm looking at has to do with my case. I'm not supposed to be anywhere near it, but I've been keeping up and taking notes. The guy in the video still hasn't been identified, but they have gotten through the layers more and more.

"Hi, my sexy detective." She closes the door behind her.

I glare at Carmella and point the pen I have in my hand at her. "Sergeant. And not your sexy anything. We're done. Get it through your head. Now, get out."

She pouts. Usually, those sultry lips would have me rock solid in nanoseconds, but not this time. "Don't you even want to know why I came?"

"I don't care why you came. We have nothing to say to each other. Remember, you're the one who walked."

She sighs dramatically, the pout still on her lips. "Can't you just hear me out?" She sashays her hips as she walks to the other side of my desk.

"No. I have absolutely no desire to hear you talk or explain anything."

"Cole," she almost whispers. Her lip trembles, but she quickly hides it. "I just want to apologize. Really. I messed up letting you go. I messed up again when -"

I hold up a hand. "Just save it, Carmella. I told you. It's over. I've moved on. You need to."

She finally reaches me, and it's then I see what Matt was seeing. I narrow my eyes at her as she stops next to me. "I know all of that, but I'm begging for a second chance, Cole. We've been through so much. What does she have that I don't?"

"A personality. A heart. A voice that doesn't annoy the fuck out of me. Oh, and that little thing called fucking empathy. You know. That something that kinda proves she's not a psychopath."

Carmella has the decency to look hurt as I turn in my chair and look up at her. There's something going on. She puts her hand on my shoulder. The pout turns to something a lot more sincere. "I know I fucked up, Cole. Okay? I shouldn't have left. I should've fought for us. I shouldn't have lied and tried to make people think we slept together when you were drunk, and that we were back together. I know you're with that other girl, but -"

"Just stop, Carmella. I can't fucking listen to you anymore." I finally see what has her scared.

It's a wire.

She's fucking wired. I look at her very carefully to see if there's a camera anywhere that stands out. She doesn't have any pins anywhere. I don't see buttons on her tight, green tank top. The button on her skin-tight jeans is covered by her shirt.

"Cole," she whispers as she shakes her head. Her eyes are wide with fear, and I know she's figured out I know. It's barely visible, but it's there along the inseam on the left side of her tank top.

I quickly think of a way to ask her if she's got a camera on her without actually asking. I glance at my laptop. It's still open, but I made sure nothing was on the screen when she came in. "You can't do this, Carmella. You can't show up here. You could get me caught with Dylan. She's already going to question me when Matt tells her you were here. Not only that," I tap the camera on my laptop as I close it, "there's cameras everywhere." I look at her questioningly as I turn back around in my chair.

She, thankfully, understands what I'm asking and shakes her head as she bites her lip. "I know, Cole, but I just… I couldn't wait to see you. And you don't answer my calls or texts."

"That's because I can't be caught. It's no secret I'm not over you. Why the fuck do you think I was drinking like that? Go lock the door." I nod to the door. I need her to play along.

"I wish you would've told me that in the hospital." She locks the door and hurries back to me as I'm writing directions on my notepad.

"With my entire family around? Are you out of your mind? I might be coldhearted and a complete asshole, but I'm not fucking heartless. I'm not going to hurt Dylan like that." I show her the note I wrote. It's telling her to make sounds like we're fucking when I tell her to, but not to let me remove her shirt.

She nods. "So, you're saying that I'm just going to be a side piece."

"Yep. My terms. You want me, that's what's happening. Maybe later on down the road, things will be different, but right now, you're a good fuck and nothing more. Agree or get out."

"Okay. I agree. Whatever you want as long as I have the opportunity to prove to you that I'm more than just a good fuck."

"I'll agree. Now, come here. Dylan's not giving me any. Something about her cheerleading bullshit and needing to be on her game."

"Anything you want, Cole."

I hold out an arm and have her sit on my lap, showing her another note that tells her she needs to be hugging me and moving so it sounds like she's straddling me and moving against me. "When the fuck have I ever let you call me by my name when I've fucked you?"

"I'm sorry, sir," she purrs, slipping right into the role I need her to play.

I position her arms so they're around my neck. "Good girl," I rumble against her skin to sound muffled.

Like a pro, she kisses her arm and hides her face in it as she makes the kinds of sounds I want her to. While she's doing that, I text Josh and all of the guys in our family in our group chat. We created it a while ago to keep our work from other family stuff. We have a chat for our whole family, too.

Cole: Carmella is in my office. She's wired. Something is fucked up. She's terrified of someone, but can't tell me without being heard. I'm bringing her to your house, Josh, but we'll be coming in hot. I'll confirm, but I think she's being followed. Should I show I found the wire, or not?

I'm inclined to not lead on I've found the wire, but I want outside judgment. This is an extremely delicate situation.

I moan against Carmella's shoulder and move enough to make noise against the wire just as Josh answers.

Josh: No. Fuck no. Something big is going down. Grab both of your teams and follow her wherever she goes, but let her go right now. Do not come here. Follow her. She's going to lead us to the fucker we want. When she gets wherever she's going, raid the house like you're doing a warrant. Extract her. Search her like you normally would. Remove the wire. Arrest her and the other person who will be there. It's Ethan.

I almost lose my cool, but cover my gasp with a low rumble instead. "Good girl. Just like that. You know how I like it."

"Mmm… Yes, sir." She rubs against me faster, causing more friction for the wire to hear.

Cole: What the fuck? You want us to go in with just our team? What the hell is going on? What are we up against?"

Dane: Good question. What are we doing, Lucinio?"

Josh: I'll explain everything later. Go in like you normally would. Make the arrest on both of them. Bring them back to the department.

Ryan: Josh and I will meet you there with Robby. He'll drop fake booking files for them both, but they're coming with us. She's in real fucking danger and needs protection. Something huge is happening. Follow orders.

Robby: Just landing now. Someone's gonna have to come get me.

Gavin: On it.

"Fuck," I rumble as I text the same word to the group before putting my phone down. Time to make this believable. I grip the hem of her tank top and start pulling up. "Get rid of the shirt," I growl.

She grips my wrist. "No!" she squeaks quietly.

I slap her ass. "I wasn't asking. Don't disobey me again." I start pulling up the shirt, and breathe a sigh of relief when she jerks up and fights me.

"Cole, no. No, please? I... didn't expect this here and now. I... um... I'm not proud of the bra I'm wearing. It's a sports bra and kinda ratty. I know you like when I present myself better than that. I'm sorry, baby. Please don't be mad."

I grin and wink at her. She's making me out to be an even bigger asshole than I am. I've never said anything like that to her before, but she's playing this out exactly how she needs to. It's almost like her life is on the line.

"Why do you do this shit to me? Huh?"

"Cole," she rasps like I'm choking her. I grin because it's a really nice touch. Makes me seem a lot more dangerous and unhinged than I am. "You're hurting me."

"Get off me. Get your fucking shorts back on. The next time we're together, you better follow my rules."

"Yes, sir. I'm sorry," she whispers as she gets up.

I put a finger to my lips and show her the texts so she can see the plan. "Go straight home, Carmella. I'll meet you there later after I tell Dylan I'll be late."

"I... was supposed to meet a friend for dinner," she says quietly.

"Did I say that was okay?"

"I'm so sorry, sir. We made the plans before all of this. If I don't show up, she might kill herself. She's going through a lot."

I sigh and groan. "Fine. I have some shit to do anyway. I'll meet you at eleven, but we need to be quick. I don't want to fuck things up with Dylan. It would cause a lot of problems with me, and you know I don't like problems."

"Yes, sir. We'll be discreet."

I stand and lead her to the door after putting my phone in my pocket. "Good girl. Now get the fuck out. Don't say a damn word to anyone." I open the door.

"What do I do?" she mouths.

"Go to Ethan," I mouth back. "Don't leave until you see me. I'll follow. Trust me."

149

She studies me for a few moments before she nods and starts to leave the office. She hugs herself and puts her head down. Matt is already gearing up. Dane hands me my gear, and I put it on as I follow him and Taylor and the rest of our teams out.

"What do you make of this?" Nick asks me, his voice low.

"I don't know, man. I trust Josh and Ryan know something we don't. All I know is if she was wired and told to come here to seduce me, this is bigger than I understand. She's smart. She wore tight clothes on purpose. She knew I'd see the damn wire. The question is who the hell is behind all of it?"

"Taylor talked to Ryan a little bit ago. I guess Ethan is leading us right to him. He said something about this just took a huge fucking turn."

"Trap?" I ask.

"I don't think so. If it were, we'd be going in with the mafia. This is our own operation. Taylor has legit warrants and everything."

We make sure to stay far enough behind Carmella so that our voices can't be picked up. She leaves through the front of the building where I assume she parked. We all head directly for our vehicles. Once I have my earpiece in place and connected to everyone else, I pull out of my parking place.

"I'll lead. I told her to look for me before she takes off." I drive around the building as everyone acknowledges me and see her parked near the corner.

She's looking around nervously, but once she sees me, I watch her almost instantly calm. I let her pull out. I follow but allow a few cars in front of me. If she trusts me as much as I hope she does, despite our breakup and history, she'll know I'm close and watching her. I might not want anything to do with her, but I'm not going to let her get hurt.

I just don't like going into something like this blind...

Chapter Nineteen

☂ Dylan ☂

I watch as Josh and Ryan march Carmella and the man I now know as Ethan Lucinio past us. I look at Dallas and Rosie in utter shock. "What's happening?" I whisper.

Dallas clears her throat. "From what Josh said, everything changed… I'm assuming this is what he meant."

Rosie crosses her arms across her chest. "I don't understand any of this, and I really wish my dads were here."

I put an arm around her. Dallas follows my lead, and we both hug her to our side. Gavin comes in, followed by Luke, Ryan's second in command. After them, an entire line of people start coming in from both the Crane and Lucinio families. Some of them I don't even know. They spread out. Some head outside, where it seems that all of the women are going, while others head for Josh's office. The three of us stand frozen.

A few moments later, Alec comes in with my dad, a man I've discovered is his second in command and two other people who are close to him. He makes eye contact with Dallas as one person and my dad stand next to him. The others go outside.

"Alec?" Dallas whispers. "Aero?" She looks up at the other man.

Alec doesn't hesitate to hug her as the other man, Aero, stops, waiting for Alec. "I just need to check in with Josh. Go outside with the others," Alec says. All three of us seem to relax a little bit at the direction and guidance he provides.

"Why are all of these people here?" I finally manage to ask.

Dad puts his arm around me and Rosie. "Something huge is happening, sweetheart. Let's go outside. We'll get the information out there. Josh's house is big, but not that big. Not for this."

I swallow hard and turn to follow him, but my eye catches Cole walking through the door. Dane heads for Josh's office, but Cole's eyes meet mine. I pause. Dad glances at Cole before leading Dallas and Rosie outside.

Cole takes a deep breath and takes my hand. "We need to talk, princess."

My heart sinks. My chest gets tight. I follow him, but I feel like he's carrying me. "Uh oh," I whisper. Cole closes the door to a room that looks like a playroom for Josh's son, but it must be being remodeled or something because it looks like it could be an office. Cole leads me to a couch and pulls me into his lap. "Are you going to break up with me?" I look down at my lap.

"What?"

"Because whatever it is that annoys you about me -"

"Dylan, I'm not breaking up with you, baby." His large hand cups my cheek. I close my eyes and sink into him in relief. "Why the hell would you think that?" He turns my face to look at him.

"I don't know. It's just been a crazy day. I'm all over the place with emotions right now."

Cole wraps his arms around me and snuggles me as close to him as he can. Just like that, all of the noise in my head quiets. The confusion. The fear. It's like I'm in a crowded room, but all I see and hear is him. Like his aura is my shield.

After a few moments, he gives me a gentle squeeze and kisses my neck. "What happened, beautiful?"

I breathe out into his neck. "My practice went super well, but then a football player told Austin that there was someone waiting. With the field lockdown and not needing so many people there with the new agreement with the school and everything, we all decided to be escorted out by Ben

152

and Landon plus the entire football and cheerleading teams. And... it... was a good thing that was the decision because it was Ethan, and he was there alone. With a letter and my money."

Cole furrows his brows. "What?"

"Yeah. All of it. Every single dollar. I didn't see the letter, but Ben said that there was stuff in there that proved everything he was saying. He kept saying stuff about his boss. It threw us all because I didn't think he had one."

"Not if he's the leader of RW. He's the boss."

"Yeah. He kept talking about his boss. He was so fucking calm and collected, Cole. It was scary. He reminded me of Josh. Just... more heartless. I don't know how to describe it. There was no emotion. Ben just said everything is about to change right before he let him go."

"That seems to be a common denominator."

Cole nuzzles my neck before kissing it. "I have something to tell you, and I don't know how you're gonna take it." He hugs me tighter before meeting my eyes. "So, I'm gonna lead this with I don't want to be with anyone else. You're it for me, Dylan." He leans in and kisses me, but it's different this time. It still has the same spark, but it's like he's pouring his soul into this one.

My eyes flutter closed, and my body molds itself to his like it's the flame I need to survive. "Mmm...," I moan into the kiss.

He slowly pulls away but keeps me as close as he can as he looks down. "Carmella came to the department today. She was wearing a wire, and I don't know where the feed was leading. Robby is working on it right now, but we don't know why she was wired. We don't know what the purpose of it was. All we know is that Ethan did it because he had his orders. That's what he told us after we arrested him."

"You arrested him?" I tilt my head. "See, this is... everything, all of it is confusing. How are we even here?"

Cole chuckles. "Okay. For me, it started with shit not making sense. Things I've already told you. The account number. All of that. I was looking into it. I'm just hitting dead ends. I needed quiet, so I grabbed a vacant office. Matt came in and talked it out with me a little before telling me Carmella was there, and she was scared. She was intentionally wearing tight clothing. Usually when she's out, she looks very professional just in case she's seen and recognized. She came onto me pretty hard, and at first,

I was telling her to leave until I saw the look in her eyes. She really was scared. Matt wasn't fucking around."

I nod slowly. "I think I know where you're going with this."

"I figured out pretty quickly that she wasn't wearing a camera. It was all audio, but she did confirm there wasn't a camera. I thought it was Ethan. It would make sense, given what he said on the phone about taking me out and going down the line to destroy Josh. I played along. I told her to make sounds like I was fucking her, and she played the part as well as I hoped she would. She even made me sound like the biggest asshole and abusive. Like she was afraid of me. That was great because it makes me sound a lot more dangerous than I am. I was trying to figure out how the hell to get her out of it and texted Josh, but over the wire it sounded like we were having sex, and I stopped it in the most asshole way possible. I made it sound like I'm planning to cheat on you and carry on this relationship, but that was never the plan. I needed to buy time. I planned on finding the wire but decided it was best to check with Josh first. And before you say anything, trust me when I say I know exactly how that sounds."

I clutch my stomach and let out a breath. "It sounds like you're trying to cover your ass if it comes out."

"I know. I know that's how it sounds, baby, but I need you to trust that I'm not like that. I may be a lot of things, but a cheater is absolutely not one of them. I'm in love with you, Dylan. I've -"

I look up at him. "You're in love with me?" I whisper.

His eyes swim with emotions I can't even identify, but the one shining through the most is the one that I didn't dare dream of.

Love.

Pure love.

Something he's shown, but not this powerfully.

He rests his head against my forehead. His hand caresses its way up to the back of my neck, and he squeezes just enough to pull me a little more into him. "For the first time in my thirty-six years, yeah. I'm in love with you." His amber eyes glow.

I feel like I'm flying. That the only thing keeping me grounded is him. "I'm in love with you, too," I whisper.

"I swear, Dylan. Nothing that was recorded was anything like it sounds," he whispers back to me.

I nod and hug him tightly. "I trust you," I say into his neck as I close my eyes.

Tension in his shoulders releases with the breath he lets out. He buries his face in my neck and hugs me even tighter. "I really thought you were going to leave me for this. I went with instinct, and when it was all said and done, I started thinking about you and how you'd feel if that got out somewhere."

I smile into his neck and inhale his clean, masculine scent. "I might be young, but I don't think I'm that immature. I do trust you, and I know sometimes your job requires unconventional methods. You knew she was in danger, so you played into what was obviously wanted."

"You're so fucking smart, baby," Cole whispers as someone knocks on the door.

"Cole, let's go. Just found out a lot of bullshit," Dane says when he pokes his head in.

"Coming," Cole rumbles. He kisses me and nudges me up. "I really want to figure out all of this shit right now, but I feel like that might be wishful thinking." He takes my hand as I sigh.

"I think the biggest issue for me right now is all of the unanswered questions. I don't even know what to feel. So much has happened. I feel like the only thing keeping me anchored in any manner at all is you."

He chuckles as he leads me out of the room. "We've come pretty far, haven't we?"

That makes me giggle. "From you being an insufferable asshole? The guy who stole the bedroom when any gentleman would've given it to the damsel in distress?"

He laughs and nods. "You make it sound like I was really awful."

"Uh. Yeah. You were."

I hear a voice clear just as we're walking outside into Josh's backyard. Everyone is gathered around the pool. Josh and Alex are standing near Ethan. The resemblance between them is striking. Ethan definitely has darker skin. A person can see the Mexican American in him, but it's impossible to deny the obvious relation to Josh and Alex.

I turn towards the person who cleared her throat, and take a deep breath. Carmella. She takes a visible deep breath. "Can we talk for a minute?" Her voice is meek. Almost like she's been completely beaten down.

"No. There's nothing to say," Cole says. He starts walking again, still holding my hand, but I gently tug it free.

I smile up at him. "It's okay. I'll meet you over there."

He glares at Carmella who looks at the ground. "Fine. But -"

"Cole. It's okay. I can handle it." I look him directly in his eyes and see the overwhelming sense of pride he feels as he nods. He shoots Carmella a last withering look before turning and stalking towards the others. I fold my arms over my chest. "Okay. What?"

"Look, I know I'm not your favorite person, and I deserve it, but I wanted to tell you this personally before you find out with all of the others." She scrubs a hand down her face. "I was being blackmailed ever since the day Cole called me over to his house to talk when he was drunk." She looks at me pleadingly as I narrow my eyes. "It was the perfect time. My job was to get back together with him and watch him. Get as much information as I could about everything going on with this case with Ethan."

"Wait, so Ethan was blackmailing you?"

She shakes her head. "No. He wasn't. I was being blackmailed by a man I didn't know the name of. I was to do what I was told to or be killed in a very violent and inhumane way that was described in grave detail to me. I was sent pictures that were photoshopped of me depicting all of the ways it would be done. And to make it all sink in, he had someone following me all of the time. He made sure I'd see him standing outside my house. He followed me very obviously."

I bite my lip. "I'm so sorry. I don't know what to say. That's awful."

"It was. And when I failed the first time, I had to regroup because my life was on the line, and I had to beg for it. I only had one chance. That's when Ethan showed up. We came up with the plan that I'd go to Cole. What we didn't expect was him to be ordered to wire me. The boss wanted to hear everything so he knew I wasn't going to Cole for help, which was what my plan was. I just had to figure out how. I came up with the idea to wear the tightest possible clothing I could find so Cole would see the wire. I wanted him to find it so I had an out. I told all of this to Josh already. I'm sure he's filling everyone else in right now, but this is personal to you. I just... want you to know that I never would have done this if I didn't have to. You don't have to believe me. You don't know me.

I don't expect you to believe anything I say, but I hope that you do and can understand."

It takes me a few moments. I can hear Josh talking to everyone. He's telling them everything Carmella is saying to me in private. "I feel like everything that's about to be said is going to take a lot for us all to process."

"Yeah. You're telling me." She hugs herself. "I'm not really sure all he told you, but what happened in his office was absolutely nothing. I had to make it believable to save my own life. I would've done whatever Cole said to do anyway, but this time, I'm so glad he chose to make it sound like we were back together. I got a call when I was driving to Ethan's house from the boss. He was very impressed and told me to keep on Cole because he thought he was getting close to unraveling everything."

"You don't know who the boss is?"

"Um... well, I... didn't... Not then. I do know now because Ethan told Josh, but I was sworn to secrecy when I asked to speak with you privately. Josh... thinks it would be best if everyone heard everything at the same time."

I eye her suspiciously but decide Josh is probably right. "Okay. Well, I just want you to know that I understand and forgive you, but I can't say I'm no longer angry. I think you could've been honest with us all in the hospital. Especially Josh. Hell, only Josh if that's what you wanted. I think he could've helped you then."

"Hindsight is twenty-twenty," she says softly as she puts her hand on my arm and gently squeezes before letting go just as quickly. "We should get over there. My part in this was small. I'm sure he's waiting." She puts her head down and hurries to stand near Josh.

I follow, a sinking feeling settling itself in the pit of my gut. When I burrow in Cole's arms, my back to his chest as he leans against the wall of the house, and see the laptop that Josh sets up on a table he puts next to him, that sinking feeling grows.

My cousins.

They're all sitting together with Colton and Blade, the president of Texas' chapter of Viper's Venom. Tears sting my eyes, and I wish like hell I could just curl into them. I miss them like crazy, but seeing them makes all of this so very real.

Josh doesn't need to say a word...

… I already know who 'the boss' is…

Chapter Twenty

❦ Cole ❦

I watch Josh set up his laptop and feel the very second that everyone, especially Dylan, figures everything out.

"Shit," I whisper.

Dylan covers her mouth. She turns to me and buries her face in my arm. "Oh my God."

Everyone murmurs something, curse words, phrases of disbelief, and utter shock. Dallas and Rosie wrap around Dylan. Raleigh, Skyla, Lyric, and Harleigh surround her for support. Jessa, Dani, Breetana, Arianna, and Nicole all follow suit, and it's now that I realize just how close all of these women are. How supportive of each other they are. I've seen this before, but it never really sank in until today when my girl was the one needing the support. It all hits me right in the heart.

Josh clears his throat. "I assume you all just figured out what I brought you together to talk about. We spent quite a while believing our enemy was Ethan Lucinio, our family. Brother. We have definitive proof, all of the missing pieces, that Ethan isn't the one we're after. In fact, I just got word that the person we are after is on his way here with his wife." Josh pauses as the girls, still forming a protective bubble around my girl, move aside just so she can see Josh and her cousins. "Foster and Mackenzie Remington."

I hear something break and glance over to see Ink by himself. His back is turned to everyone and his hand is up to his head. The glass shattered against the wall enclosing the yard is a dead giveaway that he's just as pissed as I am. Mackenzie is his ex and mother of his child, but I don't think he's ever going to forgive her for all she's done, right down to taking his kid and his whole life away by faking her own kidnapping, leading him to believe she and their child might actually be dead.

He leans against the wall with his forearms pressed against it as Ethan takes over. "Listen. I know a lot of you are probably wondering why the hell you should trust me, and I don't blame any of you. I made sure a lot of shit that went down led right to me, but my reasoning was always the same. Protect my family. Live the way my father wanted me to. I know a lot of you hate Matthew Lucinio, and you all have your reasons. I'm not going to invalidate any of you. I can tell you honestly, he knew he fucked up. He knew his life was going to come to an end, and he knew how it was going down. There was never any other option that he saw for himself no matter what I said or pleaded with him to do. Everything changed the second he found out about Jaxon."

"How did he know?" Lyric asks. "I want to know. It's an answer I never got."

"It's a good question. The answer might not be what you're expecting. It might piss you off, and that's okay. You're entitled to think whatever you want. I know all of his transgressions. I don't condone any of them and never have. I never will. The answer is he knew about you and Josh. He was watching the Crane's and Lucinio's very closely. He truly hated you all. He had his reasons. It all stemmed back to him getting his entire future ripped away from him by his father the day he forced him to marry a woman he'd never met. He lost his love that day. He lost his son. He knew she was pregnant. He knew when Nick was born. He saw him a few times when he was a baby, but ended up staying away when his father threatened both Nick's and Nick's mother's life. He kept his eyes on her, though. He planned to go back to her when his father died, but that didn't happen either. He got word that his father had hired someone to kill her, her husband, and Nick. He was trying to protect them, but his father found out about his plans. Rebekkah tried to tell my father that she heard all of

160

the plans, but my father was already implementing his own to stop his father. That's where it all stemmed. He blamed his father. He blamed the Crane's for agreeing to the deal with the marriage for peace between them. And then he blamed his kids for outsmarting him. He was watching them. He learned about you."

"So, he found out I was pregnant…," Lyric whispers. She sits down in DJ's lap. He wraps around her and pulls her tightly to him. Matt puts his arm around both of them.

"Yeah. He did. And it all changed. You were an innocent in all of this. You reminded him of his long lost love, just as Jessa did. The difference was his change of heart. He saw you to Josh as he saw his own love for Nick's mother. I guess it was different because Josh was his own flesh and blood. That's when he came to me and told me to help protect you. He had a lot of enemies. He never knew where they were coming from." Ethan looks at Josh. "And this right here is where my story is going to differ from what you heard."

"Yeah. I already saw that coming." Josh sits next to me. I pat him on the shoulder as Dallas snuggles right into his lap. He puts his arms around her and cuddles her as close as he can.

Ethan plunges along. "This was before Aero's time. He relayed what he heard from others, and that was that I went against Matthew and took Jaxon. I didn't. Jaxon was taken from under me and my watch by men who were under my command, but they didn't do this under my orders. I spent three years looking for Jaxon."

"Thank God we brought the kids to Rebekkah's and Kent's," Taylor says as he hugs Nikki. I've never been so grateful either.

"Come here, baby," I say lowly to Dylan. I've been letting the girls comfort her, though she's been in my lap the whole time, but I know she needs me more right now. She doesn't hesitate to curl up as small as she possibly can in my lap. I engulf her, hugging her tight.

Ethan takes a breath. "Matthew was killed during that time, and just after that is when everything changed for me." He pauses and glances at the screen of the computer before looking away and meeting Alec's eyes before he looks at all of us. "I have a son. I adopted him when he was a baby. My father actually saved him. He busted some of his guys doing a lot of drug dealing. He was in a house where meth was being cooked. He had lung issues that we were, thankfully, able to cure by getting him out of the house. He was only six months old. My father was going to adopt him himself, but he saw the bond I formed pretty quickly with him. He became mine. He's seven now. Lively as ever. The problem is that two years ago, the very day I found Jaxon, my son was taken from school. I found out when I went to pick him up. He wasn't there."

"Oh my God," Dylan murmurs in my chest. I run my fingers through her hair and kiss her head.

"Father was gone. I wasn't coming to you guys. I wasn't clean myself. Maybe that was a mistake I made. I don't know, but it didn't matter because that day, I knew I was in over my head. I knew I had to do all I could to lead you to me so you could take out Foster. He's the one who had my little boy taken. He's the one who had Jaxon. I didn't know how. I didn't know any of that until he called me and told me the only way I'd see my little boy again was to play his game."

"And you did. With no hesitation," Alec says.

"You're right. For a little while until I could figure shit out and gather information. I had to keep up appearances. I let everyone believe I was the bad guy. I let photos of me with the nurse who helped kidnap Jaxon be created. The photos were already there. She was a wild child. All that needed to be done was photoshop me into them. Didn't take a lot to do. I let Foster spread the narrative he wanted. Anything to protect my little boy. By the time he did all he wanted and knew I'd play along, he'd let me see him, but never have him. To this day, he's still dangling him over my head."

"So wait," Aero interrupts. "I joined you around that time. None of what you're saying makes any sense with what I found and saw."

"Everything you saw, Aero, was under orders. I wasn't the leader of Ruthless Warriors. Not until Foster brought me in. I was the leader of what was left of my father's mafia. Foster renamed us Ruthless Warriors. Franklin and his dick brother coming after Harleigh and Raleigh was all based on shit my father set up long ago to keep Josh on his toes and lead him to me. Which he did because he knew I was trying to find his grandson. He had no idea how much shit would change. The stuff you found was all stuff Foster planted along with stuff that I threw in because I knew you were a good guy who would come to them. I had Skyla kidnapped because I knew she was connected to here. I had to set something up to get you in. That's why I made you stay with Skyla and her asshole ex in the hideout. It's why I sent you on the ship with Jaxon so you could see him and make sure he was okay. I couldn't be the one to do it because I was being watched very closely by Foster."

"What about my life and my kid, Ethan?" Aero asks. "You threw us under the bus to save yourself. You could have been honest with me."

"Aero, no. I couldn't. And I never fucking threw you under the bus. I made sure your wife and daughter were safe. I knew exactly where they were, but made you believe it was all me so you'd lead them to me. I knew they'd figure it all out and save us both. But your wife fucked all of that up. She went to Foster. I still don't know how the hell she knew about him. He had to have made himself known to her. That night she called him after she tried to poison you? That was Foster. She was under orders to always say my name with him. I was sitting right there unable to do a damn thing because he had a gun pointed right at my son. I haven't seen him since that night, and that's when my plan kicked into high fucking gear. I had to speed things up."

"Jesus Christ," Alec rumbles. "Where's your son now?"

"On the way here," Josh says. "Along with Aero's ex."

"What?" I ask as I turn to him. Dylan grips my shirt.

"That note. It was coordinates to where Foster was," Josh says. "I had a team hit them at the same time you hit Ethan and Carmella. Lucky for us, Aero's wife was with them. They're on the way here."

"My son," Ethan says with a half smile, "was being held not far from them. Last I heard, the team just picked him up and are on the way here in a different jet."

"Well, before we question him, I have a question," I say. "What the fuck does Dylan have to do with any of this? He told her -"

"That he had some trouble when he was younger with Matthew Lucinio, and she was to be his when she was sixteen, but then that deal became mine?"

Dylan glances up at me before him then back at me before she hides back in my chest. I can tell she's already done with all of this. She just wants it to end. "Yeah."

"That was never my deal. That was something he came up with on his own. I think he thought it would keep me in line. After he took my son, I was his. He knew that. He'd already gotten to my guys anyway and put in a few of his own, then made me the leader of Ruthless Warriors, which was the few guys I was in command of from what was left of my father's mafia. Just rebranded with a different name. Everything he did made him money. He was into some very dirty and corrupt bullshit. I integrated into Viper's Venom under the guise that I was looking for ways to combine with them and take over." He looks at Blade on the screen. "I became rogue when Foster got too close to my real plan. So, I told him that the only way to take you out and combine to become more powerful was to come out publicly as the leader of Ruthless Warriors. Until then, I was officially, but I had people as fronts to hide my identity. That was under his orders."

"You criss-crossed the state spelling your name so we'd know it was you," Blade says with a chuckle.

"I thought it was pretty smart. I didn't expect it would take you guys forever to come after me." Ethan chuckles. "I get it, though. You were hitting dead ends not put in place by me. I learned pretty quickly that Foster knew more than he was letting me believe."

"How did we end up with Jaxon?" Josh asks. "Seems like every piece of information we've gotten and any leeway we made was all put in place by you somehow. We thought it was Matthew's lawyer."

"It was me. I was the person you all thought was the lawyer. All a figment of my own imagination. The letters. All of the hints. It traced to one of my aliases, but I never connected that alias to me. If I'd continued with it instead of changing things, you'd know it was me by now. I knew every move you'd make. I knew when I had to leave because it was all set up by me. Jaxon, though. That wasn't me. That was Foster. I didn't know what he was doing or why, but no one on that cargo ship is alive anymore because I had orders to kill them. Which I did. Happily. The shit they did was fucking heinous."

"So, Foster just had a change of heart?" I ask. "That makes little sense."

"I guess that's a question for him. I suspect he needed you off my back for a little while, though, because that was around the time everything started with Dylan. Not that he'd be marrying her off to me, but it was coming to the end of her time in Texas. He started mobilizing people up here. He had me rent an apartment up here close to the hotel she was supposed to be at. The problem with that was that it allowed him to keep my son at a further distance. I'd had enough. That's when I made the decision to really start going after you."

"The video of Cole," Carmella says softly.

Ethan glances at her. "Yeah. It was all a set up. I tried to make it as obvious as possible. I set the camera up. I knocked out a cop. Stole his uniform and car. He woke up in the hospital with no recollection of what happened. I set up the camera. During the edit, I used AI to give myself a new face. I tried to do a good job while making it seem obvious it was an edit. I didn't realize it would take so long to peel layers. I don't know how that shit works. And before anyone says anything about the guy I killed, I chose him because he's one of Foster's men and beats his wife and kids."

"Why didn't you just say something to me, man?" Blade asks. "You were still there when we had Alec down there for that shit we were being framed for."

Ethan chuckles and looks at the screen with a raised eyebrow. "Ever wonder why you were framed in the first place?"

Alec chirps out a humorless laugh. "Son of a bitch. Foster."

"Yep. You guys were close to ruining his business. Trafficking. Drugs. Guns. Gambling. All the people he bought off in the department. The people who came with me when I left were all people on his payroll. They knew as soon as Alec got involved that their time would be up. Everything leads back to Foster. Everything. That flashdrive I gave to Dylan's bodyguard proves it all. There's picture documentation that's backed up on the flashdrive. He wasn't smart enough to hide his paper trail. And Dylan. Sweetheart, I'm sorry for everything with him, but the account that he set up for your college fund was put in place for him to escape with. He has several offshore accounts. He took off because I told him Josh was coming for him. I told him to get my son to safety. I did that because I needed your suspicions on him. I needed you after him so I could put my own plan into place."

"You had my mother with you," Dylan whispers.

"Yeah. I did. That wasn't part of my plan, but Foster played right into me. He trusted me implicitly by then. He sent his wife with me and left to his secret hideout with my son before he moved her to a different hideout. I was able to get the money back because I said I needed it for his wife to make sure I could keep her safe. When the dust settled, I sent her to him telling him it was safe, but it was perfect for me because I could use her and put your suspicions on her and your father a lot faster. The day I called you -"

"How did you get that number?" Dylan asks.

"You called your mother, baby. She had it because of that. Gave it to him," I tell her.

"What about me?" Rosie asks quietly. "Ruthless Warriors killed my grandparents."

"Again. Not me, sweetheart. That was Foster himself. Your grandparents knew too much about his operation. They'd contacted the FBI. That's why the FBI was involved in investigating their murder. I don't know how close they got to you or if you were even questioned, but I know they didn't get anywhere with the case without their testimony. What I do know is that your mom got in trouble and sold you. I didn't have to do anything at all with that. I was very hands off. You were already involved with your dads. I left everything alone with that. The only thing I did was give the person responsible more ammo about it not being over. That there was still a bigger boss out there. I believed he gave you my message. Especially when we went after Skyla." His eyes meet everyone's. "Any other questions?"

"Yeah," I say. "What happens to you now? Why Carmella?"

"Carmella wasn't approached by me. She was blackmailed by Foster. The only reason she's still alive is because I promised her I'd get her out from under him as long as she played the game exactly as I told her to. She did. She went to you just as I told her to. And got the message to you just like she needed to. Foster called when she left and said everything was perfect. He heard everything. I couldn't relay that to her, though, until she got to my house. She was still wired, but I know he called her because she wrote that on paper for me. We sat there after that and waited for you guys to bust in. Josh said after we met up the attack was completely coordinated."

"I still don't see how we're all supposed to trust you," Gavin growls.

"Simple. You don't. Trust is earned. I know I have to earn it as much as everyone else has. I have a lot of work ahead of me. That's on me. You have Foster now, and I'm willing to stick around. I'll do whatever it takes to prove myself."

"Right answer," Gavin says with a nod.

Dylan hugs me a little tighter, and I kiss her head. "I want to confront them," she whispers.

"You'll get your time," I whisper back.

Rosie gets up and hurries into the house. She's the only one out here who doesn't have someone comforting her. I start to get up and go after her with Dylan, but I see Ink is watching her. After a few moments, and what looks like a war with himself, Ink goes after her.

"This is finally coming to an end," Josh rumbles.

"Yeah. Finally," I agree as Dylan slowly moves from my embrace. She takes the laptop and moves to a private corner with it. I smile because through all of the shit, she knows she still has family, even if they aren't blood.

It may be almost over, but there are still a lot of loose ends.

Loose ends we need to tie up right now.

Starting with Carmella.

Chapter Twenty One

☙ Dylan ❧

It's been hours since Ethan revealed so much. More than I think any of us could really process, or even fathom.

"I have so many questions," I mumble to Cole on the way to the interrogation house. I've never been there, but Josh texted Cole and asked him to come now before things with my parents got ugly. I assume that means before Josh gets his hands on them.

"So do I, princess." He hugs me to his side as we walk the last few steps to the house.

Before he even has a chance to start pushing in codes, Josh opens the door. "Before you enter," he starts, looking directly at me, "you need to know that Aero is in here and his ex didn't make it. There was no use for her after she confessed. Your parents are already pretty messed up."

I meet his eyes, my own devoid of emotion. "They're not family. I will never forgive them for all of this. They deserve everything that's coming to them." I shrug as my eyes narrow angrily. "Vigilante justice."

"Well, Foster is going down for treason. I've already arranged for a nice place in hell for him. He was making a lot of his money by selling state secrets to Russia. Lance just sent all of that information to our government contacts. We'll be delivering him with a nice bow."

I just stare at him wide-eyed. "That... actually... wow. It explains a lot. I've heard him speaking Russian sometimes and was confused."

Josh grins. "That's not even close to all. Turns out pain freaks that bastard out. He doesn't like others being in control and having any kind of power over him. If you think you'll be okay, he's ready to answer whatever questions you have."

I nod and take the hand he holds out to me. He leads me into the interrogation room, and I blink a few times. The lights are dim, but I can clearly make out three people. One of them is slumped over and covered in blood. She doesn't look alive.

I look up at Josh quizzingly. "Is she...?"

"That's Aero's wife," Josh confirms as he lets go of my hand. "Floor is yours, sweetheart."

I jump just a little at the hand on my back, but immediately recognize it as Cole's. "It's okay. Don't look at her," he whispers in my ear.

I nod in response, but I don't have to worry. My dad, my real dad, and Gavin make a barricade so I don't see her at all.

"Dylan! Baby!" my mother cries.

"Shut the fuck up, Mackenzie," my dad growls. "You know fuck well you've never wanted her. Or... was that a lie?" he sneers viciously. Her eyes widen and she shrinks against the wall she's chained to. "That's what I thought. Wouldn't want to end up like your daughter here, would you?"

I furrow my brows at him. "Her daughter...?"

"Oh, that's right, sweetheart. You don't know. Aero's wife, here, is Foster's biological daughter. Not Mackenzie's, but she definitely adopted her as her own. She's only seven years younger than Mackenzie. Abandoned by daddy, but daddy got back in her good graces the day she turned eighteen when he kidnapped her and killed her mother."

I just blink at him. "I'm so confused. How did she end up with Aero?"

"He's had his hands in many pies for a long time, honey. It was all planned." My dad looks at Foster with disgust. Foster has the decency to look down.

"Well, that's okay. My entire life was a whole fucking lie." I cross my arms over my chest as Cole puts his arm around me.

"Watch your mouth, young lady," Foster says.

"I'm sorry. You're not my father," I growl as I turn to my mother. "And you're no longer considered my mother. Not since I found out the truth. I have questions, though."

"And you're going to answer every single one," Josh says as he kneels between them. He slaps both of them in the face. They groan. "Aren't you?"

"Yes," Foster growls. Josh chuckles as he stands and leans on the metal table next to me. I didn't realize until now that it's bolted to the ground.

"First question. Why the change of heart? Why let me move here if I was supposed to be married off to Ethan?"

"Stupid girl. Because with you marrying him, it gave me access to the Lucinio Mafia by name. I let you move here so you could feel like you beat me. Ethan was supposed to kidnap you before you even started school. But he was thwarted by that fucking riot."

"Yeah. That he caused," I say.

Foster grumbles. "Found out he betrayed me a little too late, now didn't I?"

"He was never on your side in the first place. You kidnapped his son, you sick son of a bitch," I spit.

"Would've been a lot better if your fucking friends didn't get involved."

I scoff. "Do you honestly think Ethan just, what? Backed off when Landon dropped me at the school? No. It was so obvious to me even back then that they left of their own accord. Ethan knew I was safe from you."

Foster shakes his head. "Your biggest problem is that you're too smart for your own good."

I roll my eyes. "Second question. Why? Why do all of this?"

"Do I need a reason? You were never wanted, Dylan. If I could've sacrificed you earlier I would've, but it didn't end up working out."

"Why not just sell her to Matthew when she was an infant?" Cole asks.

"Because that wasn't in my best interest. I already had a deal with him. I didn't need her for him. The only reason I started using her is because I wanted more, and he wasn't playing ball. And then when he was killed, I needed to feel out Ethan. I wasn't going to just give her up to him without having a plan."

"So, my whole life, all I've been is a pawn. And you had another daughter this whole time?"

"After my first divorce, she didn't want anything to do with me. Her mother had filled her head with lies by that time. When she turned eighteen, she sought me out."

I shake my head and turn to Cole. "I'm done. I know all I need to. There's no point in asking more questions I don't care to know the answers to."

Cole nods. "What about this treason thing I hear about?"

Foster barks out a laugh. "Russia pays more. How do you think I've been able to live how I live and do what I do?"

Cole hugs me tighter and looks at my mother. "What about you? What's your problem?"

Mackenzie glares at me, not bothering to make eye contact with Cole. "I was young. You ruined my body! I wanted to give you up long ago, but Foster didn't let me. We were going to sell you into human trafficking, but he had better ideas." She spits at my shoes.

I suck in a breath. I did actually have one more question, but I don't even want to ask now. I already have my answer. I wondered if either of them ever loved me. I know for certain there was never any love for me. It was all a lie. All of the kindness they did show was never for my benefit. It was all for show.

I break away from Cole, anger building inside me. My chest feels like it's collapsing. I turn, breaking free of Cole, and flee from the room. One of the guards makes his way to the door to let me out, but Cole beats him to it.

As soon as Cole gets it open, I run outside, angry tears running down my face. "How can they sit there and be so cruel? Heartless!" I shout.

Cole catches up to me, takes my hand, and slows me to a walk. "They're done. They're out of your life. Don't think about them anymore." He takes my hand, and it comforts me, as usual, but does nothing for the raging inferno inside me.

"I don't understand, Cole. I don't understand how I could grow up living a life of privilege. It wasn't all bad, you know. I got teased a little bit. They called me a privileged little princess. That's why I hated when you called me that until you turned it into something that I really love. Not a mockery." I look up at him. "But it wasn't really bad! How can my life not be terrible, but then have them being into so many horrible things? My dad was selling our classified information to another country, and I don't even know if that was truly the worst thing! Selling people to others like their property? Oh my God, Cole!" I shriek, losing complete control of my emotions.

"I know, baby." He squeezes my hand.

"I want to scream. I really just want to break things. Hit things. And even then, I'm not sure the rage I feel at all of this will truly be satiated."

"Believe it or not, that's completely normal."

"Not for me! I'm supposed to be cheery all of the time! Smiley. Ready to take on the world and be encouraging towards others. I feel like this dark beast is inside me trying to tear me apart from the inside out!" I kick a rock and watch it bounce off a mailbox and clatter into the street. I stomp my foot and scream because I can't stop the noise from coming out. It's been building until it felt like an explosion.

Cole squeezes my hand as Ryan meets us on the sidewalk with Carmella in front of Josh's house. Carmella's head is down like a submissive bunny just hopping along behind him.

"I know you're pissed, Dylan, but it's your decision on what happens to Carmella," Ryan says as Cole stops me.

I glare angrily at her. "Honestly, Ryan? I don't want her anywhere near us. Thank you, Carmella, for doing what's right in the end, but you still royally fucked up."

"I know," she whispers.

"I want her away from us. From all of us. Put her on a secluded island. I don't care. Just make sure it's anywhere but here, Ryan. Please," I plead.

"Pick anywhere in the world, then, Carmella," Ryan says. "Anywhere. A dream place to live if that's what you want. Nowhere in the United States. Think of it like Witness Protection because that's what's happening here. You'll need to change your name, looks, and entire identity. No news reporting. No journalism."

Carmella sniffles. "I understand."

I feel like I'm vibrating as I tug Cole towards his house. I need to not be around anyone. Maybe I need to go into his gym and start hitting his punching bag. "That might have been vindictive."

Cole laughs. "Baby, she gets to go anywhere in the damn world, all expenses paid. Ryan and Josh will even set up an account under her new name and give her an allowance each month. She'll be fine."

"Good. I guess I don't really want her to just die." I wait for Cole to open the door to his house before I storm inside. "Oh my God, Cole, I don't know what to do. I have so much pent up anger. I want to run, scream, hit something. Maybe we should go to a rage room."

"Or you could go to the gym and take it out there." Cole closes the door and spins me to face him. His mouth meets mine in a kiss that melts the ice I feel flowing through my veins. It's like lava meeting the cold ocean.

"Mmm…" Something inside me snaps. It's like I've become feral. I tug on his shirt and push it up. He takes it off and drops it on the floor. His hands are right back on my hips. He backs me against the wall and presses his lips against mine once more.

Everything changes. I'm still angry. I'm still buzzing. But Cole makes it all shift to something else. He gives me an outlet. Needing more, I hurriedly unbutton my shorts and push them and my panties down my thighs. I kick out of them as Cole strips me of my shirt. He makes quick work of my bra while I'm unbuckling his belt and working his button.

I start to push his jeans down, but he stops me with a nip to my lip as he turns me. "Can't wait anymore." He pushes me against the wall and runs a finger through my slickness.

"Oh my God." My eyes roll back, and I almost come just by his touch.

"Perfect." With no warning at all, Cole spreads his legs as he grips my left one and lifts it. He pins me and pushes his length deep into my pussy.

"Oh… Cole!" I moan.

Cole holds my leg high, like I'm doing a high kick, and thrusts hard, deep, and fast. His other arm snakes around my waist and pulls me into each of his thrusts. "Fuck, so tight. So fucking wet for me." His lips crash to mine in a punishing kiss that detonates inside me like a bomb.

There's nothing gentle. Everything I need right now, rough, is all he's giving me. Dominance. Complete control over me. I push back into him. Our already slicked skin slapping against each other makes the most delicious of sounds.

I feel myself pulsing around him. He's so long and thick that he's completely ruined me for anyone else, and that's just fine with me because I don't want anyone but him.

Like the absolute bedroom legend that he is, Cole pounds into my pussy, and I know I'm going to feel him for days. He builds up my orgasm like a firebomb. I claw at the wall, scrambling for any kind of grip before he makes me explode into a screaming mess.

"Ah!" I scream as he keeps ramming into me. "Cole! Don't stop! Don't fucking stop!"

"I wasn't planning on it," he growls against my lips.

And that's when he truly lets loose. He holds nothing back as he thrusts into me like a man starved. He pushes deep. His dick thickens inside me with every powerful glide of his silk-encased cock. My body slams against the wall as I completely submit to him.

His hand circles lightly around my neck. His thumb and forefinger grip my jaw. His amber eyes darken just before his mouth covers mine once more. His tongue thrashes against mine at the same pace of his thrusts. He nips and sucks my lower lip before crashing his tongue into my mouth again and again and again.

"Mmm!" I scream into his kiss. I get wetter and wetter. My thighs tremble. My stomach tightens. Tingles begin to spark into something more, something greater, until my whole body is shaking.

"Scream for me. Don't hold back," Cole says. His hard and cut body touches every part of me, driving me to madness.

"Ah!" I scream. "Ah, Cole!" I scream again because it feels so fucking good to do. Almost as good as his dick rutting me.

"I know you got more than that for me." He shifts his hips with each thrust as his hand moves from my neck to my clit. He starts rubbing with his thumb, setting a furious pace that has me seeing stars.

"Cole!" I scream again. "Ah!" I close my eyes and don't hold back the scream. It comes from deep within and releases all of the pent up emotions I didn't even know I still held. Cole doesn't stop pounding into me the entire time I scream.

"Now, come," Cole commands against the corner of my mouth.

"Cole!" I come so hard that the stars I see quickly turn to flashes of light, like a ball of metal when it's put into a microwave. My hips jerk into him as my pussy clamps around him and pulses just as powerfully as his thrusts.

"Dylan!" Cole shouts as jets of his come shoot from his cock deep inside me. I love that feeling. I love the feeling of him filling me, claiming me as his own.

When we finish, Cole gently lets my leg down. He slides out of me. I instantly miss the feeling of him, but not for long. He pulls me into his lap on the floor as we both pant and catch our breath.

After several moments of him running his fingers through my hair and his hand up and down my back, I finally let out a content sigh. "I'm going to marry you someday," I whisper.

Chapter Twenty Two

❦ Cole ❦

I tense at her words. Marry me? Am I really the marrying kind? I've never thought of spending the rest of my life with any other person but Dylan.

Well.

One.

One other person.

And she walked away.

"Uh…" My heart beats wildly, screaming at me to just tell her. Agree. It's not like I haven't already proved it in other ways. I've probably even said it in more ways than one. So, why the hell is this time any different?

She looks up at me questioningly, but it quickly fades to something else. Something I can't quite make sense of. She reaches up and runs her hand along my stubbled jaw. "I didn't mean to say that out loud. I'm sorry," she says quietly. Her beautiful eyes dim as she kisses me softly and stands.

And it's right there that I figure it out.

Pain.

It's pain she's feeling and trying to hide.

She starts to pick up her clothes and put them back on. I want to comfort her, but I can't find the words. I need to tell her why I am the way I am. Why I'm so fucked up. I've never mentioned it before, and it's not fair to her. She opened up to me about so much bullshit in her life that she never should've had to deal with, including being called princess as an insult by people she thought were friends.

I let out a breath and start picking up my own clothes as I stand. Dylan is quiet, and I hate it. That wasn't my intention. I wanted her to feel better after the bullshit with Foster and Mackenzie. I didn't want her to feel like shit for opening up to me like that.

Dylan starts to walk away, but I grab her arm. "Grab some water, baby," I say, my voice low.

She glances up at me with a soft smile. "It's okay. I'm not thirsty."

"It wasn't a request," I tell her, my voice changing from low to dominant. Her eyes flash, and she nods. "You need it. Especially after that."

"Okay."

I let go of her arm. She hurries to the kitchen as I cross the room and sit down. I haven't buckled my belt and have no intention to. I lean forward on the couch and rest my elbows on my knees as I drop my head into my hands. I run my fingers through my hair as I let out a long breath meant to soothe me. It doesn't do much more than cause more tightness. It's like there's a vice around my heart.

I feel Dylan sit down, but I don't move. I can't. Not yet. I see the glass she sets in front of me, and I'm grateful. I reach for the glass as she stays quiet. After gulping down half of it, I set the glass down. There's no better way to do this than to dive in head fucking first.

I lean back. Fuck it. Time to rip off the bandaid. "When I graduated from college, I had a girlfriend. I was head over heels. I was planning to propose and everything."

Dylan stays hunched over as she peels the label from the water bottle in her hands. "I see."

I chuckle. "I wish you did, baby. It would make this a lot easier, but it's not what you think. See, there was a pretty big issue that she had, and it was something I wasn't willing to budge on. And her name was Jessa."

She glances at me at that point with furrowed brows. "Jessa Crane?"

"Yep. She was Jessa Holloway then. And she was Alex Lucinio's girlfriend, or so we thought. They were taking things slow even though they lived together, but there were problems. It started out like the perfect love story. Until red flags started popping up. We both saw a lot of issues that neither of us could figure out. It was like Alex had a switch in his mind that would flip, and he'd be a completely different person. I started to suspect that Alex was really Josh, but I didn't know. When I brought them up to Jess, she kind of brushed it off, but I knew shit bothered her. It was because of that reason that I convinced her to stay with me. Alex, or Josh, as we now know, was pissed about that."

"I remember some of that. He went after her."

"He did. But during all of this time, I was dating someone, and we were serious. She wanted to move in, but she wouldn't with Jessa there. And I wouldn't make Jessa leave because I was all she had. We were best friends. There was nothing we wouldn't do for each other, but it stopped there with us. We were mature. We'd dated briefly, but decided we were a lot better friends, so that's what we stayed. When Josh put Jessa in the hospital, my girlfriend took that as her sign to move in. She thought if she moved in, I wouldn't kick her out or let Jessa back."

"But that didn't exactly happen?"

"Well, kind of. I didn't let Jessa back, but the reasoning was because we needed to get her out of LA. We moved her to New York, and I took a leave of absence. I didn't think anything of it. My girlfriend didn't agree. I invited her to New York with me, but she refused. She didn't think I should be going off with another girl, but Jessa was and still is family to me. I wasn't going to abandon her in her time of need. Looking back, I wouldn't have made any other decision than what I did because I know it was the right one, but then, the break up fucked me up. We tried the long distance thing, but Jessa was always a source of contention for us. I hated that my girlfriend couldn't trust me, and she hated that she thought I was stringing her along. In the end, we broke up. It wasn't very amicable, and I spent a lot of time blaming myself for it and second guessing every fucking decision I'd made. Was it right to choose my friend, my family, over her? Should I have just let Jessa go? She did a pretty good job at making me feel like everything I did was wrong."

Dylan shifts on the couch until she's facing me. She crosses her legs and puts her hands in her lap still holding the water bottle. "So, you broke up because you chose a woman who is like family to you over your relationship?"

"At the time, that's how I saw it. Now, it's more I made the decision to -" I cut myself with a shake of my head. "Yeah. There's no explaining that one away."

"The way I see it is Jessa needed you, and your girlfriend didn't understand. That's not your fault. It's hers. I guess a lot of people would be saying differently, like you wanted to spend your life with her, so you should've chosen her, but to me, I don't think like that. Jessa didn't have anyone, and she needed help. I never would've faulted you for that. I would've been on the first plane out with you to help her. She needed you just as much as she needed to know that she had a support system outside of you."

"Well, I'm glad you think that. It was pretty devastating for me at that point. I had the ring and everything. By the time it was all said and done, I decided my family was more important to me than anything else. Marriage, though? I didn't think I was cut out for it. If I could leave her without a second thought to be with family, am I really able to commit to a marriage? It was honest torture. It still is. If faced with that situation again, I'd still choose family." I look at her sadly and lightly caress her cheek. She leans into my hand. "What kind of man does that make me?"

Dylan reaches up and grips my wrist. She turns and kisses the palm of my hand before bringing my hand down and holding it in her lap. "I think you're not really seeing the bigger picture here."

I chuckle dryly. "And what's that?"

"Well, maybe it was never really love. You've made several sacrifices for me and thought about me, but really, I don't think that's what it is. You've separated her in your mind from your family and think that when it comes to us, you'll choose family over me because that's what you did with her. But what if this time it's different? What if in your mind, I'm not really separated from family? What if I'm just as important and held at the same level as them? And what if it was never like that before because you were never really in love before?"

I look down at my lap as she plays with my fingers. It takes me a few moments to gather my thoughts enough to realize that she might be right. What if this whole time I've had this line between girlfriend and family because I never really considered my girlfriend anything more than that? What if the reason I'm so comfortable with Dylan and have admitted that I love her, even told her as much, is because she's more to me than any of the others? What if the reason I see a future with her is because she's my one true love, my happily ever after; my fairytale?

"Maybe you're right," I finally tell her.

"I think I might be onto something, honestly. She didn't want to make any kind of sacrifices for you. It seems to me that she wanted all of your attention. If I'm understanding, you might have been all Jessa really had, but I think she was all you had, too. Family wise, that is. If it were me in that situation, I could never dream of coming between your family and you. I would hate everything about that. Sacrifices in love have to come from both sides. She wasn't willing to make any from her side and expected you to. When you didn't, she showed her true colors. I don't really think that you were in the wrong. I just think you haven't found the right one."

I look at her and move my hand so my fingers are more able to grasp hers. I bring her hand to my lips and kiss it. "Wise beyond your years."

She blushes a beautiful shade of pink and looks down at her lap again. "I have my moments."

I let go of her hand and put an arm around her instead. I pull her close and drop a hand on her thigh. She curls her body into mine and lays her head on my shoulder. "Hadn't."

She looks up at me curiously. "What?"

"Hadn't. You said you don't think I've found the right one. You used the word haven't. I haven't found the right one. The correct word to use is hadn't. I hadn't found the right one." I hug her closer and look down at her as I rub her thigh. "Until I found you."

"Oh…," she whispers. Her eyes brighten and brim with tears of happiness at what I'm saying.

"I want to spend the rest of my life with you. I know I've probably uttered those words before, but I've never said anything like what you did. Truth is, though, I do want to marry you. Someday. I can't imagine my world without you in it, and that's not something I've never thought about anyone before. No one except family." I wait for those words to sink in.

Finally, Dylan's eyes widen, and her lips tremble. "Oh my God. Cole…" She hugs me tight and buries her face in my neck.

I can't help but pull her as close as possible and sway gently. "You're just as important as my family. You're my family," I rumble against her neck before kissing it.

She gasps out a happy sob and kisses my neck. "I love you. I love you so much."

"I love you, too," I whisper, but there's no missing the raw emotion behind the words. There's no denying the way my heart feels like it's going to burst in my chest with how full it feels.

"Actually, um… I… have something to show you." She untangles herself from me and reaches for the sketchbook she left on the table. She picks it up and holds it in her lap as she looks up at me. After taking a deep breath, she sets it in mine.

I raise an eyebrow as I look down at it. "What am I doing with this?"

"I want you to look at it," she says softly, looking down at it in my lap.

I glance at her. "Baby, you said you've never let anyone look at your sketchbook. You don't have to show me if you don't want to."

"I want to." She meets my eyes, hers sparkling with pride and shining with love.

I grin and look down at the book again. "You sure?"

"Mmhmm." She reaches over and confidently flips the cover up.

"Holy shit." Revealed on the first page is the sun rising over the lake, but the drawing is so realistic; the colors so brilliant that it feels like I'm sitting right on the lakeshore. I look at her. "This is really fucking good. You know Nick's wife is an artist?"

She blushes. "Dani Jade. She's brilliant with a camera. I started drawing by copying her photographs. When I got my technique down, I worked on my own drawings." She flips the page since I'm mesmerized by her talent. The next one shows buildings that were around the penthouse and the streets below with cars.

"Jesus. The detail." I flip to the next page. It's more abstract, but it almost looks like she sped up camera speed or something and drew traffic on Chicago's I-90, but all that's on the paper is streaks of light amidst tall skyscrapers.

181

I continue to flip through. There's a variety of drawings that range from landscapes to people. She drew each of her cousins and Dallas and Rosie together with herself. She drew everyone in the Crane and Lucinio family, but there's one that strikes me the most.

Several.

Several of them make me emotional.

Me.

She's drawn several of me. Me working out. Me cooking. Me staring pensively out the window. Me napping.

But my personal favorite has me looking at her teary. I point to it. "Why would you want to remember this?" I ask her. It's me in the hospital with a machine breathing for me and hooked up to another machine that's feeding me.

She smiles a little sadly and points to herself in the photo. "Because of that."

I furrow my brows. "Tears?"

"No... That."

I pay more attention to what she's pointing at. Our hands. I look closer at her and see she's smiling. It's sad, and she's crying, but our hands are linked. "It looks like I'm holding your hand. But how? I was unconscious."

She carefully takes her sketchbook and puts it down on the table. She snuggles into me once more and rests her head on my shoulder. I hold her as tightly as I can. "You were. But... when I sat down next to you, it was almost like you knew I was there. Your hand kind of twitched. I put mine in yours and held your hand, but little by little, your fingers started curling around mine. It was like you knew, subconsciously, that I was there with you. And you wanted me to know that you could feel me. I drew it because that's what kept me going for the four days after that before they made the decision to wake you."

I gently shift her and stand. She looks at me a little shocked and slightly worried, but I bend and lift her in my arms. I carry her up the stairs to our bedroom, kissing her lovingly the entire way. Once I get us to the room, I kick the door closed behind me and set her down.

Without a word, the two of us get ready for bed. We don't need to say anything. The emotion we're both feeling is thick in the air, and I want her in my arms before I dare speak.

After a few minutes, we both crawl into the bed. Once she's settled, I bury my face in her hair and kiss her neck as I hug her tightly against my body with no intention of ever letting her go. "Thank you for showing me your sketchbook," I whisper against her neck again as she melts against me.

"You're welcome," she whispers. "Thank you for telling me about your ex."

"I love you, princess," I whisper.

I feel her shift so she's even closer to me. Like I'm engulfing her. "I love you, too, my love."

I kiss her head and let myself drift with her. From being accused of murder to the riot and everything that came after, the past couple of months have felt like a lot longer. It doesn't feel like it's only been a summer since my life turned upside down and then was righted once more by the woman curled so naturally into my side.

I have no idea what the future holds for me, but what I do know is that with my girl by my side, I can handle anything that comes my way.

Me and my girl.

I love how that sounds.

Chapter Twenty Three

❦ Dylan ❦

(One Month Later)

When I first learned that some of my favorite people never went to their Prom, I decided there absolutely had to be a redo. And for those who did get to go, I decided it was mandatory they got to spend it with the people they love so deeply.

I finish stapling the last strand of white lights to the edge of Cole's house. Our house. I bite my lip and smile shyly as I look down at him.

"Done up there?"

"Mmhmm." I start to climb down.

"Good." I feel his hands on my hips, and he lifts me the rest of the way down. I giggle when my feet touch the ground, and he turns me around to kiss me. "Tell me again why this is so important?" He grins teasingly as he pulls away.

I swat him with a giggle as I pull away. "Because everyone deserves the perfect Prom and the perfect Prom kiss."

He laughs as he follows me. "The perfect Prom kiss? What is that?"

I turn to him in shock. "It's when you kiss your date at the perfect time, making the whole night perfect."

His grin turns cocky. "Ah. And did you get your perfect Prom kiss?" He grabs me again and tugs me close.

I giggle. "No. Because you weren't there." I wrap my arms around his shoulders and wait for his lips to meet mine. Only right when they're about to meet, Rebekkah and Kent come into the backyard with their two adorable kids, Jordan and Harper.

"Okay, kids. Put us to work," Kent says.

Cole groans. "Awful timing," he says, his voice low.

I smile and kiss his jaw before turning to Kent and Rebekkah. "First, we need the food set up on the table. I don't want to bring the cake out until later."

"We're on the food!" Rebekkah says. She brings the kids inside with her as Kent follows.

"Okay. We're running out of time," I say to Cole. "Where is the DJ? Wasn't he just here?"

"He went to the bathroom. And the caterers have left already, but I'm pretty sure they left the serving staff. They're just waiting on orders from the boss."

"I could really use Lyric for this, but I refuse to let her do any work. I want her to enjoy herself."

Cole chuckles. "Good luck with that, princess. She isn't good with just relaxing."

"Well, tonight she is. End of story." My eyes scan the yard. The dance floor is set up just at the privacy wall that separates Cole's yard from the rest of the property.

"I think it's time we go get dressed. The others should be here soon."

"Just a minute…"

Tablecloths are perfect. All silver. The centerpieces, a vase filled with tall, pristine, and fresh Blue Passion Flowers, set off the tranquility I'm going for. Strings of pretty white lights line the entire area. My theme, tropical, pops out at every single corner all the way down to the Lily of the Valley flowers that line the lights and the Birds of Paradise palm trees that line the dance floor. I've asked the girls to wear something fancy they'd wear to a fancy dinner anywhere tropical. I've asked the guys to wear black slacks, dressy shoes, and something they'd wear to a fancy dinner anywhere tropical. The hope is all of the guys will match their dates somehow.

"Okay. Let's go. Out of time." Cole grabs me around the waist and throws me over his shoulder. He marches into the house.

I laugh. "Okay! Okay! Put me down."

"Nope! No chance of you escaping this way." He slaps my ass, making me jerk into him with a groan as my eyes roll back in my head.

"Not fair."

"Not fair that I know how much you like that? Or not fair that I'm bigger than you and can do things like this?"

I laugh. "None of it's fair."

"Well, I don't play fair." He bites my ass on the way up the stairs, and I squeak. "You should know that by now."

I giggle as he puts me down in the bedroom. "I do know that. So, how are we going to do this?"

He raises an eyebrow. "Do… what?"

I put my hands on my hips. "I want you to see me in my dress at the perfect moment."

He laughs. "Isn't that a wedding thing?"

"Well, yeah. I guess. I just wanted you to see me when I was coming down the stairs, though."

"I've already seen your dress, baby."

"But not on me."

He holds up his hands with a grin. "Okay. I'll grab my stuff and get dressed downstairs."

I jump up and down clapping. "Yay!"

"You're fucking adorable, and I'm going to get my fill of you later. I hope you know that." He says it so calmly as he grabs his outfit that I stop cold and just stare at him. He turns and winks at me before he leaves the room.

"Yep. He's going to be the death of me." I shake my head, trying to rid the thoughts of me pinned against the door he just exited while he pounds his length into me. "Jesus Christ." The man makes me hot.

A few minutes later, I'm dressed and ready to go. I sneak out of the bedroom and hide behind a wall to look down the stairs. I don't see him right away, but when he steps into view, he takes my breath away. Cole doesn't dress up often, but when he does, he puts others to shame.

He's wearing shiny, black dress shoes to match his black pants. His shirt is white and long-sleeved, but he's rolled them up, showing off arm porn. To adhere to the tropical theme, the shirt is adorned with Proteas, a tropical pink and orange flower to match those that are printed all over my white, floor-length, silk, strapless sundress. My heels, though only a couple of inches, are the same shade as the flowers and strap around my lower calf just above my ankle.

I take a deep breath as he looks at his watch. I step out and pause at the top of the stairs. When he doesn't look up right away, I start slowly walking down the stairs, gracefully caressing the railing with my fingertips. He finally looks up when I'm a few steps down, and I smile as he sucks in a breath.

"You were right. I'm glad you made me wait for this moment." His voice is husky and filled with sexy possessiveness. I love that I'm all his.

"You don't look so bad yourself, handsome." I smile softly when I reach him. He takes my hand in his and kisses it.

When his eyes meet mine, I melt. He grins the sexy, cocky smile that makes me weak in the knees. "Our guests should be arriving soon. Ready to get them laid?" He wiggles his eyebrows, his amber eyes showing amusement.

I crack up. "Cole!"

He laughs and leads me the rest of the way down the stairs and to the door. He opens it as I take the homemade leis and place them over my arm. It doesn't take long before Lyric shows up with Matt, DJ, Beckett, and Layne. I smile brightly and give them each a lei before sending them outside. Behind them is Mariah, but she looks very down.

"You okay?" Cole asks, looking over her head. "Where's Luca?"

"Oh. Um." She looks over her shoulder. "He had something come up." She looks back at us with a smile, but it's so forced and fake that it breaks my heart.

"Well, that's okay!" I smile cheerfully. "We'll have fun without him!" I give her a lei and send her outside, but I'm worried. I don't think things have been going too well for her and Luca lately. My smile gets brighter when I see Rosie coming with Lance and Damon. "Yay! You made it!" I give them each a lei.

"Wouldn't miss it! This is going to be amazing!" She kisses my cheek and hurries outside excitedly.

Cole grins and waits until she's no longer in earshot. "You think she's going to crush on your dad all night?"

My eyes widen, and I playfully slap his arm. "Stop it!"

Cole laughs. We continue to welcome everyone who shows up, including Zeke. I squeak happily when I see Roman, Zeke's four-year-old son and Jaxon's new best friend with him. I squeal excitedly when the next to arrive are Landon and Ben. I begged them both to come. I give away my last lei to Ryan and turn to head outside with everyone else, but Cole stops me. "Just a sec." He opens the closet and takes out five more leis I didn't know he had.

"Where did those come from?"

"Well, they're for them." He points outside and steps next to me as one of Josh's SUVs pull into the driveway.

"Oh my God!" I nearly shout when I see my cousins step out. "Oh my God!" I don't wait for them to walk to the door. Instead, I run to them, meeting them by the SUV. "Oh my God! What are you guys doing here?" I throw my arms around Xavier. Brant, Drake, Kody, and Sterling all gather around us laughing.

"Cole invited us. He thought you might miss us or something," Sterling says.

"Oh my God, I can't believe this!" I turn and hug each of them, but I don't need to with how tightly they're all gripping me. "Where is everyone else?" I look up at Xavier as Cole meets us in the driveway.

"Well, Colton is working on a big case with Blade," Drake answers.

"And Sloane had a huge opportunity in New York to meet with the *New York Times* about a story she'll be able to work independently on. She gets to see her friend, Jason, so she's happy." Brant grins.

"That's amazing! Her career is just shooting to the stars." I smile proudly.

"I couldn't be more proud. And with Jason there, I know she's in good hands."

"Well, let's get you guys leid and out back," Cole says with a grin. Everyone laughs as he holds up the leis. I can't wait until Cole and I spring our surprise on everyone.

ॐ ॐ ॐ

Hours later, after everyone has had their fill of food and danced until they can't anymore, I take in the scene. Ryan and Arianna are still slow dancing as their son, Chris, holds onto Ryan's leg, while standing on his foot so he can dance, too. I've never seen a more peaceful looking couple. Ryan might be a busy man, but he's all about his family. They always come first, and I love that so much.

Jason is rubbing Jessa's feet while their son, Nate, lies with his head on Jason's thigh. Alex and his wife, Raleigh, are in some kind of game of tag with Zeke, Luke, Robby, Dane, and Skyla. Tait, Jordan, Harper, Roman, Zeke's son, and Zane, Ethan's son, are working hard to keep up with adults in their game of tag. Chase and Breetana are laughing over drinks with Gavin and Harleigh. Josh and Dallas are being adorable in their own piece of heaven in a corner of the dance floor. Jaxon looks like he's about to pass out but refuses because he's having too much fun with Beckett, Layne, Alec, and Mariah.

"Do you think there's something going on with Rosie and my dad?" I ask suddenly. "I mean, really. Joking aside."

Cole kisses my shoulder. "I don't think so, baby. He noticed she was kind of off being a loner and asked her to dance earlier. I overheard that. But she also danced with Ben and Landon. Even me."

"She lit up, though, when my dad asked her."

"Well, she lit up when I asked her, too, princess. I think she was just happy to be included. She danced with each of your cousins and Ethan. I think she danced with everyone here."

"Yeah. I guess you're right." I lay my head on his shoulder and yawn. "This was such a good day."

"Agreed," Taylor says from next to us. He's running his fingers through Nicole's hair. Nick is rubbing Dani's back on the other side of us.

"I think after everything we've been through over the past eight years, this was definitely something we all needed." Nick smiles at me. "Thank you for putting this on."

"Oh, I'm not done yet." I lean over and kiss his cheek as I pull Cole up with me. I lead him to the DJ.

"We're really doing this?"

"Oh yes."

"You sure?"

"Yep."

"You realize you're going to make Skyla's entire fucking life. And Dallas is going to kiss the ground you walk on."

I giggle. "I do." I smile up at him, my eyes twinkling. "I love the way those words feel on my lips."

"You know what I like the feel of on my lips?" Cole gives me a wicked grin. His eyes seem to light on fire.

I blush furiously. "Cole!" I whisper-scold him. He just smiles even more as I turn to Lyric.

"The envelope, madam." She gives me a bright smile after handing it to me before she goes and curls into Matt's lap. DJ takes her hand, resting his other on Matt's thigh and grins at me as our DJ gives me the microphone and stops the music.

I clear my throat. Cole wraps his arms around my waist. "Everyone? We have an announcement."

Cole pulls something out of his pocket and slips it on my finger. A few people gasp. My cousins all applaud when they see the ring. "We got engaged last night and have a pretty big surprise for everyone. It's been in the works for," Cole looks at his watch, "well, hours."

Ethan, who just got back a few days ago from settling Carmella in the South of France, gives me a wink of encouragement. It's only been a little while, but he's already become one of my favorite people.

"Alright, spit it out, kid!" Josh says from the other side of the dance floor where he's still hugging Dallas. Jaxon giggles and holds his arms up for him. He picks him up, and they all watch me intently.

Today is the perfect day to do this. Foster was tried for treason against our country and convicted, but in a huge turn of events, it was also discovered that he also committed treason against Russia. They've asked for him to stand trial in their country, and the United States, surprisingly, agreed. He was flown to Russia and starts his trial with them this very week. He'll spend life in prison in Russia. The best the United States could do was twenty-five years with a chance at parole after fifteen. Russian prisons aren't known for being kind. He gets his new beginning, and we get ours.

I open the envelope and look up at Cole. He kisses me, and I feel like with him at my side, nothing can stop me. "Next summer," I begin, "I'm super excited to announce that we're all going on a vacation. But not just any vacation." I turn to Josh.

On my cue, he drops to one knee in front of Dallas. He smiles up at her, still holding Jaxon with one arm. He holds up a small box for Dallas and flicks it open with his thumb to reveal a ring he's been holding onto for a couple of months. Dallas' hands fly to her face, and she covers her mouth.

"Oh my God," she chokes out.

"Dallas, you know how long I've been in love with you, baby. I can't imagine my life without you in it. As Cole so eloquently put it when we were both agonizing about it maybe being too soon to propose... When you know, you know. And I know I want to marry you. So, what do you say? Will you marry me?"

"And me!" Jaxon says. Josh looks at him with a grin.

Dallas laughs and nods her head. "I'll happily marry you." She boops Jaxon's nose. "And you." She bends to hug Josh, but he stands up so she can hug both him and Jaxon.

DJ and Matt chuckle with large smiles as Lyric squeaks excitedly and claps her hands happily. "Finally!"

"This vacation," I begin again, quieting everyone's applause after a few moments, "is one for the books."

"With three weddings," Cole finishes for me, his eyes locked on Dane's.

Dane grins. "We thought we could get married with Cole and Dylan and Josh and Dallas."

"A triple wedding!" Alec laughs. He's standing so close to Mariah, and she's smiling so happily for once, that I can't help but really want the two of them to get their own happy ending. "I fucking love it!"

"I have tickets and everything in this envelope." I wave it in front of me. "But they're just for us couples to go and plan our wedding."

"However, in case any of you are wondering why Dylan picked this theme, it's because she wants to use the money she got from Foster to treat the entire family to a trip to Mustique Island in the West Indies. Where we will also be getting married. Meaning, the trip and the wedding is on us."

"Wow," Sterling breathes. "Fuck, I've always wanted to go there."

"Well, you're in luck, cousin of mine. Because you get to go next summer." I smile barely able to contain my excitement.

Like a firework, everyone bursts into cheers and starts hugging each other. Even Rosie and Mariah seem happy as they join in the celebration.

"I think we did good," Cole rumbles against my neck as he wraps his arms around me from behind.

"Me too."

Cole sways gently with me as we watch everyone. We need this. We all need a breather after everything that's happened over the past eight years. I may not have been a part of all of it, but I'm a part of this amazing family now, and I can feel how badly everyone needs a break.

They're going to get it. I'll be damned if they don't. They deserve it. We all do.

As everyone lets loose in a second burst of energy, our makeshift Prom is back in full swing. It's nice to see everyone let loose. It's even better to see a peace settle over us. I know instinctively it's a feeling that will be long lasting and hasn't been felt for so long.

The Lucinio and Crane families have grown over the years, combined, and have become a fortress built on loyalty, respect, and most importantly, love. A family that will only continue to get stronger through each generation.

I'm honored to be a part of it and can't wait to see what comes next.

The End

Coming Soon...

The Viper's Venom Series

The sinfully seductive Viper's Venom Series will be coming to you Spring of 2025!

Family.
Loyalty.
Respect.
Honor.
Love.

Though tragedy and tribulations have rocked Viper's Venom to its core, this motorcycle crew refuses to kneel for anyone. They didn't become the largest and most feared crew in the entirety of the United States of America by chance.

Alec Cassidy, the man who leads this vicious crew, is just as stubborn, hard headed, and as much of a bad boy as every member of his gang.

Follow these ruthless, tough, and devilishly sinful, dirty-talking men as they navigate their way through love, loss, and betrayal to claim their heart's desire.

Coming Soon!

The Lucinio Family Series

Available Now

Rising From The Ashes
The Player's Rebel
Encrypting My Heart
Fighting My Fate
Phoenix Rising

Other Books By Melony Ann
The Beautiful Dream Series

Available Now

Loving You
My Love, My Heart
Softening Lyric
Undercover Temptations
Captain Charming
Breaking Boundaries
Crashing Into You
Tactical Inferno
Ravishing Our Queen
Cherished By The Texan
Unveiling Our Passions

Box Sets Available

The Beautiful Dream Series: Box Set: Part 1
The Beautiful Dream Series: Box Set: Part 2

The Crane Family Series

Available Now

The Reluctant Mafia King
Sweet Lies
Billion Dollar Love Story
Be Mine
Protecting Her
Dangerously Forbidden Love
His Heart
Love In The Dark

Box Sets Available

The Crane Family Series

The Deimos Trilogy

Available Now

Connor's Legacy
Aryan's Alpha
Kade's Redemption

Box Sets Available

The Deimos Trilogy

The Forbidden Temptation Series

Available Now

The Detective's Forbidden Temptation
The Running Back's Forbidden Temptation

Multi Author Series
Piper Falls: Firehouse 49

Available Now

Ignite My Fire by Melony Ann
Regain My Fire by Kindra White
Playing With My Fire by D.L. Howe
Fight My Fire by Darley Collins
Against My Fire by Anneke Boshoff
Relight My Fire by Louise Murchie
Harness My Fire by Ayana Lisbet
Quench My Fire by Havana Wilder

Let's Be Friends

Follow me on

Bookbub

Facebook

Goodreads

Instagram

Tik Tok

Visit my website
www.melonyannauthor.com

Subscribe to my newsletter and get a FREE never-seen-before NOVELLA
just for subscribers!
https://www.melonyannauthor.com/exclusive-content

Join my Facebook Reader Group!
Melony Ann's Sizzling Book Nook

The official Lucinio Family Series Playlist on YouTube
https://youtube.com/playlist?list=PLGEiD5wbQmDdjFYhMKrFsomQOTr
RK7x9Y

Dedication

To the self-centered pricks with a problem in our lives whom we love with all of our heart anyway.

Acknowledgements

Brad - Sometimes, those magical late night conversations are all a person needs to become sane once more. I love you.

Laura - All of the late nights we shared while this book was being written should be memorialized in a museum. I love you.

Jay - There are no words in this universe to describe the level of your guidance and how much it means to me. I love you.

Anneke - As you are all of the time, you've proven to be even more amazing than before. I'm in awe of you. I love you.

Jason - This book wouldn't be a thing without you and your inspiration. Thank you for being my best friend and ass-kicker when I need a boost. I love you.

Kayla - I tried really hard to go a bit more asshole with Cole for you. I hope you love him as much as me, and thank you for pushing me to dive deep with him and explore my abilities more. I love you.

To the Bookstagram Community.

To my family.

To all of those who believe in me and support me.

To all of those who don't.

Cover by: Carter Cover Designs

Edited by: Alyssa Skaggs

About Melony Ann

Melony Ann began writing short stories and poetry as a child. She continued honing her craft over the years until she took the plunge and began publishing her work, despite having severe anxiety.

Melony writes contemporary romance stories that are full of suspense and a lot of steam.

When she isn't writing, she is loving her family and working to make her life something she deserves.

Melony believes that if her writing can inspire just one person, then all of her hard work is worth it.

Her hope is that her writing allows each and every one of her readers to escape for a little while. To dive into a different world one book at a time.

www.ingramcontent.com/pod-product-compliance
Lightning Source LLC
Chambersburg PA
CBHW070504260626
47161CB00004B/1444